ANNE M(

DEATH OF A HEAVENLY TWIN

ANNE Morice, *née* Felicity Shaw, was born in Kent in 1916.

Her mother Muriel Rose was the natural daughter of Rebecca Gould and Charles Morice. Muriel Rose married a Kentish doctor, and they had a daughter, Elizabeth. Muriel Rose's three later daughters—Angela, Felicity and Yvonne—were fathered by playwright Frederick Lonsdale.

Felicity's older sister Angela became an actress, married actor and theatrical agent Robin Fox, and produced England's Fox acting dynasty, including her sons Edward and James and grandchildren Laurence, Jack, Emilia and Freddie.

Felicity went to work in the office of the GPO Film Unit. There Felicity met and married documentarian Alexander Shaw. They had three children and lived in various countries.

Felicity wrote two well-received novels in the 1950's, but did not publish again until successfully launching her Tessa Crichton mystery series in 1970, buying a house in Hambleden, near Henley-on-Thames, on the proceeds. Her last novel was published a year after her death at the age of seventy-three on May 18th, 1989.

BY ANNE MORICE
and available from Dean Street Press

ANNE MORICE

DEATH OF A HEAVENLY TWIN

With an introduction and afterword by
Curtis Evans

DEAN STREET PRESS

Published by Dean Street Press 2021

Copyright © 1974 Anne Morice

Introduction & Afterword © 2021 Curtis Evans

All Rights Reserved

First published in 1974 by Macmillan

Cover by DSP

ISBN 978 1 914150 01 2

www.deanstreetpress.co.uk

INTRODUCTION

BY 1970 the Golden Age of detective fiction, which had dawned in splendor a half-century earlier in 1920, seemingly had sunk into shadow like the sun at eventide. There were still a few old bodies from those early, glittering days who practiced the fine art of finely clued murder, to be sure, but in most cases the hands of those murderously talented individuals were growing increasingly infirm. Queen of Crime Agatha Christie, now eighty years old, retained her bestselling status around the world, but surely no one could have deluded herself into thinking that the novel *Passenger to Frankfurt*, the author's 1970 "Christie for Christmas" (which publishers for want of a better word dubbed "an Extravaganza") was prime Christie—or, indeed, anything remotely close to it. Similarly, two other old crime masters, Americans John Dickson Carr and Ellery Queen (comparative striplings in their sixties), both published detective novels that year, but both books were notably weak efforts on their parts. Agatha Christie's American counterpart in terms of work productivity and worldwide sales, Erle Stanley Gardner, creator of Perry Mason, published nothing at all that year, having passed away in March at the age of eighty. Admittedly such old-timers as Rex Stout, Ngaio Marsh, Michael Innes and Gladys Mitchell were still playing the game with some of their old élan, but in truth their glory days had fallen behind them as well. Others, like Margery Allingham and John Street, had died within the last few years or, like Anthony Gilbert, Nicholas Blake, Leo Bruce and Christopher Bush, soon would expire or become debilitated. Decidedly in 1970—a year which saw the trials of the Manson family and the Chicago Seven, assorted bombings, kidnappings and plane hijackings by such terroristic entities as the Weathermen, the Red Army, the PLO and the FLQ, the American invasion of Cambodia and the Kent State shootings and the drug overdose deaths of Jimi Hendrix and Janis Joplin—leisure readers now more than ever stood in need of the intelligent escapism which classic crime fiction provided. Yet the old order in crime fiction, like that in world politics and society, seemed irrevocably to be washing away in a bloody tide of violent anarchy and all round uncouthness.

Or was it? Old values have a way of persisting. Even as the generation which produced the glorious detective fiction of the Golden Age finally began exiting the crime scene, a new generation of younger puzzle adepts had arisen, not to take the esteemed places of their elders, but to contribute their own worthy efforts to the rarefied field of fair play murder. Among these writers were P.D. James, Ruth Rendell, Emma Lathen, Patricia Moyes, H.R.F. Keating, Catherine Aird, Joyce Porter, Margaret Yorke, Elizabeth Lemarchand, Reginald Hill, Peter Lovesey and the author whom you are perusing now, Anne Morice (1916-1989). Morice, who like Yorke, Lovesey and Hill debuted as a mystery writer in 1970, was lavishly welcomed by critics in the United Kingdom (she was not published in the United States until 1974) upon the publication of her first mystery, *Death in the Grand Manor*, which suggestively and anachronistically was subtitled not an "extravaganza," but a novel of detection. Fittingly the book was lauded by no less than seemingly permanently retired Golden Age stalwarts Edmund Crispin and Francis Iles (aka Anthony Berkeley Cox). Crispin deemed Morice's debut puzzler "a charming whodunit . . . full of unforced buoyance" and prescribed it as a "remedy for existentialist gloom," while Iles, who would pass away at the age of seventy-seven less than six months after penning his review, found the novel a "most attractive lightweight," adding enthusiastically: "[E]ntertainingly written, it provides a modern version of the classical type of detective story. I was much taken with the cheerful young narrator . . . and I think most readers will feel the same way. Warmly recommended." Similarly, Maurice Richardson, who, although not a crime writer, had reviewed crime fiction for decades at the *London Observer*, lavished praise upon Morice's maiden mystery: "Entrancingly fresh and lively whodunit. . . . Excellent dialogue. . . . Much superior to the average effort to lighten the detective story."

With such a critical sendoff, it is no surprise that Anne Morice's crime fiction took flight on the wings of its bracing mirth. Over the next two decades twenty-five Anne Morice mysteries were published (the last of them post-humously), at the rate of one or two year. Twenty-three of these concerned the investigations of Tessa Crichton, a charming young actress who always manages to cross paths with murder, while two, written at the end of her career, detail cases of Detective Superintendent "Tubby" Wiseman. In 1976 Morice along with Margaret Yorke was chosen to become a member of Britain's prestigious Detection Club, preceding Ruth Rendell by a year, while in the 1980s her books were included in Bantam's superlative paperback "Murder Most British" series, which included luminaries from both present and past like Rendell, Yorke, Margery Allingham, Patricia Wentworth, Christianna Brand, Eliza-beth Ferrars, Catherine Aird, Margaret Erskine, Marian Babson, Dorothy Simpson, June Thomson and last, but most certainly not least, the Queen of Crime herself, Agatha Christie. In 1974, when Morice's fifth Tessa Crichton detec-tive novel, *Death of a Dutiful Daughter*, was picked up in the United States, the author's work again was received with acclaim, with reviewers emphasizing the author's cozy traditionalism (though the term "cozy" had not then come into common use in reference to traditional English and American mysteries). In his notice of Morice's *Death of a Wedding Guest* (1976), "Newgate Callendar" (aka classical music critic Harold C. Schoenberg), Seventies crime fiction reviewer for the *New York Times Book Review*, observed that "Morice is a traditionalist, and she has no surprises [in terms of subject matter] in her latest book. What she does have, as always, is a bright and amusing style . . . [and] a general air of sophisticated writing." Perhaps a couple of reviews from Middle America—where intense Anglophilia, the dogmatic pronouncements of Raymond Chandler and Edmund Wilson notwithstanding, still ran rampant among mystery readers—best indicate the cozy criminal appeal of Anne Morice:

> Anne Morice . . . acquired me as a fan when I read her "Death and the Dutiful Daughter." In this new novel, she did not disappoint me. The same appealing female detective, Tessa Crichton, solves the mysteries on her own, which is surprising in view of the fact that Tessa is actually not a detective, but a film actress. Tessa just seems to be at places where a murder occurs, and at the most unlikely places at that . . . this time at a garden fete on the estate of a millionaire tycoon. . . . The plot is well constructed; I must confess that I, like the police, had my suspect all picked out too. I was "dead" wrong (if you will excuse the expression) because my suspect was also murdered before not too many pages turned. . . . This is not a blood-curdling, chilling mystery; it is amusing and light, but Miss Morice writes in a

polished and intelligent manner, providing pleasure and entertainment. (Rose Levine Isaacson, review of *Death of a Heavenly Twin*, *Jackson Mississippi Clarion-Ledger*, 18 August 1974)

I like English mysteries because the victims are always rotten people who deserve to die. Anne Morice, like Ngaio Marsh et al., writes tongue in cheek but with great care. It is always a joy to read English at its glorious best. (Sally Edwards, "Ever-So British, This Tale," review of *Killing with Kindness*, *Charlotte North Carolina Observer*, 10 April 1975)

While it is true that Anne Morice's mysteries most frequently take place at country villages and estates, surely the quintessence of modern cozy mystery settings, there is a pleasing tartness to Tessa's narration and the brittle, epigrammatic dialogue which reminds me of the Golden Age Crime Queens (particularly Ngaio Marsh) and, to part from mystery for a moment, English playwright Noel Coward. Morice's books may be cozy but they most certainly are not cloying, nor are the sentiments which the characters express invariably "traditional." The author avoids any traces of soppiness or sentimentality and has a knack for clever turns of phrase which is characteristic of the bright young things of the Twenties and Thirties, the decades of her own youth. "Sackcloth and ashes would have been overdressing for the mood I had sunk into by then," Tessa reflects at one point in the novel *Death in the Grand Manor*. Never fear, however: nothing, not even the odd murder or two, keeps Tessa down in the dumps for long; and invariably she finds herself back on the trail of murder most foul, to the consternation of her handsome, debonair husband, Inspector Robin Price of Scotland Yard (whom she meets in the first novel in the series and has married by the second), and the exasperation of her amusingly eccentric and indolent playwright cousin, Toby Crichton, both of whom feature in almost all of the Tessa Crichton novels. Murder may not lastingly mar Tessa's equanimity, but she certainly takes her detection seriously.

Three decades now having passed since Anne Morice's crime novels were in print, fans of British mystery in both its classic and cozy forms should derive much pleasure in discovering (or rediscovering) her work in these new Dean Street Press editions and thereby passing time once again in that pleasant fictional English world where death affords us not emotional disturbance and distress but enjoyable and intelligent diversion.

Curtis Evans

CHAPTER ONE

I WAITED in the shadows, in my high suede boots and frilly dress, just outside the pool of light which illuminated one corner of the sleazy arcade, watching as he reeled forward on the balls of his feet, then sprawled head first over the pin table. Still with his back to me, so that the bullet hole below his left shoulder blade was clearly visible, he slid very slowly down on to the floor, and I held my breath as for the fifth time that afternoon Christopher Cosby breathed his last and the camera swung in for a close-up of his staring, lifeless face.

We had already wrapped up the bit where I collapsed in a whimpering heap over his dead body, which naturally came later in the sequence, and this was the last shot on the day's schedule. I was the only one left on the set with no job to perform, and had remained there simply to make sure that Kit would get it right at least once and that I could allow myself to believe that the lovely, long, free weekend was really about to begin.

There had been a pin-dropping silence during the take, and then the voice of Peter Bliss, our director, rang out loud and clear:

'Cut!'

A second later there followed the blessed words: 'Print that!' and relief flowed over us like the gentle rain from heaven upon the stage beneath.

'That was fine, Kit,' Peter went on, speaking now in a conversational tone, as he emerged from the darkness behind the camera to confer with the continuity girl. 'Absolutely bang on!'

As though it were literally connected to them by wires, the tension subsided when, one by one, the lights were doused and Kit, who had now sat up and wrapped his arms round his drawn up knees, flung them out sideways and came up on his feet in one beautifully co-ordinated, rather showing-off spring.

Peter addressed us again: 'Okay, boys and girls, ladies and gentlemen and comrades, we pack it in. Have a lovely weekend, and see you all at nine sharp on Monday.'

There was a groan from somewhere up in the rafters, echoed by laughter from the floor, and after a startled pause Peter said:

'Sorry, chaps. I forgot it was Easter. See you all at nine sharp on Tuesday.'

I gathered up the book and knitting from my chair and went over to say goodnight to him.

'Time for a drink?' he asked.

'I'd love to, Peter, but I've got a longish drive.'

An unaccountable reserve had made me hesitate to tell him where I was going, and before I could overcome it his mind had flown back to his own concerns. He was staring abstractedly at Kit, now engaged in back slapping farewells with a group of technicians, and he muttered grimly:

'God, how I hate re-takes. And I hate Bank Holidays even more. We'll all be as cold as mutton by Tuesday morning. Still, you were great, Tessa me old love, absolutely great, as always, and I think we may get by with that last one. At least he kept in his marks. Oh well, all hands to the pump on Tuesday and we may pull him through yet.'

'You will, if anyone can,' I said, laying it on a bit because he looked so harassed. 'You've coped with a lot worse than this in your time.'

He patted my shoulder. 'Bless you, love. Enjoy yourself and don't lose your shirt at Le Touquet or wherever.'

It was a second chance to tell him where I was going, but before I could take it Johnny, the assistant director, came up with some query about striking the set, and the moment was lost. I waved goodnight to them both and to the accompaniment of merry cries of 'Watch it!' and 'Mind Your Backs!' picked my way through the writhing coils of wires and cables out into the daylight and down a short passage to my dressing room which was one size larger than a match box. In view of this, it was rather annoying to find Kit Cosby already installed there and occupying the only chair.

'There isn't room for both of us in here,' I reminded him. 'Not if I'm going to change, that is; and I suppose there would be cold looks if I were to turn up at Eglinton Hall in this outfit?'

'I just looked in to see if you felt like nipping up for a quick one first?'

'No thanks. Can't we stop somewhere on the way? These boots were not made for walking, even up two flights of stairs. What I really feel like is taking them off and getting cleaned up.'

'Okay. How long?'

'Twenty minutes at the outside.'

'God, Tessa, do you really need as long as that? Oh well, whatever you say. I'll meet you by the car.'

'You can take my suitcases out of the boot and put them in yours,' I said, handing over the keys. 'That'll save a few minutes.'

He stood up, once again demonstrating that impressive grace and agility which characterised all his movements, then stopped by the door for a moment, tapping his watch with a finger nail:

'I'll see you down there at six fifty-eight precisely.'

He was wearing his secretive look and I felt certain he was really calculating that he had ample time for a couple of quick ones in the interval.

Nevertheless, he was slightly better than his word, and so was I, for it was still only ten to seven by the porter's clock when he slowed down his brand new, cream-coloured Bentley to say goodnight, before we drove through the studio gates and on to the main road.

'How far is it?' I asked.

'Forty miles, give or take. We could do it in an hour with no trouble at all, if it wasn't for going through bloody Maidenhead.'

'Can't you find a way round?'

'No, duckie, I can't. There's this little waterway known as the Thames and we have to cross it somewhere. It's as simple as that.'

'Well, don't drive like a maniac, because I'd much rather be late than dead.'

'Couldn't possibly matter less, anyway. They're much too grand to have dinner before eight thirty. I suppose you're going to feel quite at home, aren't you, my little one?'

By tacit consent, neither of us made any allusion to the day's work just completed, probably because we both knew that it accounted for his prickly mood, as well as for the fact that we should reach our destination approximately one hour late. The truth was that a quite simple shooting schedule had been dragged out to a ridiculous degree, largely through his own incompetence. It wasn't even his fault either, for the predicament of Christopher Cosby was the far from unusual one that he had soared to stardom long before he had the guns or experience to carry it.

Having spent two years at a drama school, followed by as many months in a repertory company, he had been cast in a supporting role in a film producer's idea of a working class comedy, playing a lordly nitwit, by whom the working class heroine had become temporarily dazzled. Ignoring the fact that the part happened to be one in which a cross-eyed newt could scarcely have failed, the critics had gone overboard about his performance, singling him out with one voice for the rave notice. Whether his golden looks had influenced their judgement is a guess I should not care to hazard, but they had undoubtedly accounted for the merry chink of coins at the box office. To the jubilation of all concerned, what had promised to be an unpretentious, mediocre little film had turned out to be one of the biggest money spinners of the year and, with a little help from his agent's and his own astuteness a new star was born.

For Kit's was more than just a pretty face. There was a shrewd little brain ticking away behind it, a truth which had been demonstrated in his very first press interview, in which he had claimed to be the product of a slum background, who had never set foot in a theatre until after he left school. This was a fairly bright move, since it not only made him acceptably trendy, but also carried the implication that he was a rather more talented actor than any of us might have supposed. There were those who maintained that it was also quite untrue, and that his father was a prosperous business man living in relatively posh style on the outskirts of Nottingham; and it sometimes seemed to me, particularly when he was unsure of himself, that Kit had acquired his knowledge of English neither at school nor his mother's knee, but in front of a television set. He had picked up every cliché of the mass media and was rarely able to complete even the most incoherent statement without the rider that that was what it was all about.

However, for publicity purposes, Kit's own version of his social origins met all requirements, and he had daringly followed it up by the more risky manoeuvre of becoming engaged to the third or fourth richest girl in England. Her name was Sarah Benson-Jones and it was at her family's house, a few miles north-west of Oxford, that we were now going to spend the Easter weekend.

I had only met Sarah once in my life, although I had friends who knew her better, and I confess that once had seemed enough. It may appear odd, therefore, that I should have elected to drive forty miles with a bad tempered and bickering actor in order to spend three days under her roof but it had come about through the intervention of her father.

His name was Sir Magnus Benson-Jones and he was a major tycoon, operating in the oil world among other fertile fields of tycoonery, and with powers of life and death, so I was reliably informed, over governments, corporations and petrol pump attendants in every quarter of the globe. However, contrary to the popular image normally projected by such characters, Sir Magnus was no greedy, reactionary tyrant. He was, or had succeeded in becoming, a liberal minded, culture loving humanitarian, devoting much time and money to philanthropic enterprises, of which rural conservation and racial integration were both high on the list. It was the first of these which was now taking me temporarily into his life, for on Easter Saturday the grounds of Eglinton Hall were to be given over to a combined fête, flower show and children's gymkhana, in aid of the South Midlands Conservation Society, and several weeks previously the request had come to me, via

Kit, that I should mount the platform at 3 p.m. and declare the proceedings open.

Before I could turn aside with a laughing negative, Kit had whipped out a letter from Sarah, repeating the invitation in rather less peremptory terms.

After expressing her regret that we did not meet more often, etc., she apologised for begging favours from anyone so busy as myself, etc., and hoped that I would be their guest from Thursday to Monday, in which invitation she also included my husband.

She had evidently done some homework on the last subject, for she had not only got Robin's name and rank correct but had alluded to the fact that his early days in the Force had been spent with the C.I.D. at Dedley, a mere seven miles from Eglinton Hall.

In view of this, it was not inconceivable that she also knew or would shortly find out that the week before Easter had been earmarked for one of Robin's periodic conferences with some gentlemen of the Sûreté, and he was not expected back until Saturday evening, thus ruling out any chance of my using him as an excuse to decline. This, combined with an ingrained, occasionally disastrous curiosity, eventually induced me to accept, on the understanding that I should leave on Saturday evening.

Recalling these matters, I turned to Kit, who had lapsed into a brooding silence, and said:

'It's funny about Sarah. Her letter might have been written by a retired headmistress, but I suppose she can't be a day over twenty-four?'

'Wrong. She's a day over twenty-seven.'

'Really? I wonder why she's never married? I remember her as being fairly beautiful and so on; not to mention rich and clever. And it isn't as though she had a career or anything.'

'Are you joking? She has a career which makes yours look like a bag of old beans. She took over as Dad's hostess, secretary and right hand what's-it when she was twelve and she's been at it ever since.'

'I see. And the apple of his eye, presumably?'

'Right.'

'So what a tribute to you that she has now changed her mind.'

'Oh, you know how the rich are? They only want to mix with people who are as loaded as themselves, and there aren't so many of them in the Benson-Jones bracket. Sarah could afford to marry just about anyone, but she wouldn't look at me if I wasn't pulling in thirty thousand a year.'

This was not very lover-like talk and I raised no objection when a minute later he swung across the road and drew up outside a small but affluent looking pub. Even if another drink failed to sweeten his mood, it could hardly make it sourer.

It was called the *Eglinton Arms* and the yard in front of it was divided into two sections, one half marked out as a car park and the other dotted about with tubs of hyacinths and some very new looking rustic tables and benches.

'Quite a coincidence,' I remarked, getting out of the car. 'Or are we already in Benson-Jones-land?'

'Right. The house is four miles up the road, but I need a stiffener before we go over the top.'

He got it too, in more senses than one. There was only one other car parked in the yard, so the chances of his being recognised had been fairly remote, but luckily the occupants turned out to be a cheerfully uninhibited party consisting of two girls and a young man. By means of some noisy whispering on the part of one of them, the news was relayed to the others, whereupon they all leaned back in their chairs and kept their eyes fastened on Kit for the whole ten minutes we remained in the bar.

This had an even more intoxicating effect than the double scotch which went with it, and he played up to them with a will, patting my hand, throwing himself about and laughing uproariously at nothing at all.

I was puzzled by this performance, until it began to dawn on me that his ill humour owed as much to the prospect ahead as to the humiliations he had left behind. It was the first time I had heard him speak so frankly about Sarah and her father and the underlying resentment suggested that, however much they might attract him, the riches and power of the Benson-Jones world cut him down to size even more cruelly than the thinly veiled impatience of Peter Bliss and the production unit.

It was a state of affairs which did not make the coming weekend any more alluring and as soon as we were on the road again I began pumping him about out hosts. Since I was committed to spending two days in this rather charged atmosphere, it was to my advantage to find out as much about it as I could.

'How about the other one?' I asked. 'Isn't there a sister?'

'Yeah. Name of Julie.'

Most of the fizz had gone out of him once the audience was left behind but, fortunately for me, the soothing effects of the whisky were a little more durable.

'Who lives at home with Daddy too?'

'You bet!'

'Younger?'

'By half an hour.'

'Really? Lucky for you, in a way?'

'In what way?' he asked sharply.

'Just that there'll presumably be someone to take over the reins when you and Sarah are married. I take it this Julie is the apple of his other eye?'

'Oh, sure, but basically that's not the way it is. They're supposed to be identical, but it hasn't worked out. Sarah got the brains, as well as all the luck. It's as simple as that.'

'What kind of luck?'

'Well, the thing about Julie is she's crippled. Not too seriously, but enough to make it tough.'

'Born crippled?'

'No. I imagine that wouldn't be so bad. You'd probably get adjusted easier. Julie was okay till she was around twelve. They were in Beirut or somewhere and there was this polio epidemic. The mother caught it too and died. That's when Sarah began taking over.'

'I see. And has she taken over Julie as well?'

'That's what it's all about. Prising Sarah loose from her father is uphill work, but it's nothing to the problem we have to face up to with Julie.'

I considered this for a while and then said: 'Well, there's only one answer that I can see.'

'Name it.'

He was slowing down as he spoke and immediately afterwards made a right turn between two massive red brick columns, each adorned with a sour looking stone griffin perched on top. The one on the left had part of its beak chipped off, which struck me as vaguely symbolic.

I had been about to suggest that Kit should abandon all idea of removing Sarah from the parental roof and should simply join the circus and live under it himself. However, we were now within sight of Eglinton Hall, at the end of quarter of a mile of straight, tarmac drive, and I had second thoughts. Permanent residence in such a ghoulish, castellated pile was not a fate I would have wished on my worst enemy.

CHAPTER TWO

SARAH met us at the front door, which was a late copy of the entrance to a thirteenth-century abbey and plentifully adorned with cast iron bands and spikes. Unlike the house, she was a pleasure to look at, having a pure oval face, high forehead, huge dark eyes and very white teeth. She also had good manners and greeted me effusively before flinging herself into the arms of her beloved. She was almost as tall as he, about five feet nine or ten, and her movements had some of the same athletic grace. Except for the contrast in colouring, they could have passed for brother and sister.

She was wearing a maroon Thai silk tunic and trousers which did plenty for a figure which could have got by without any assistance at all. As it happened, I also possessed a Thai silk tunic and trousers which I was rather proud of but there and then rejected the idea of sporting them around at Eglinton Hall. As I have often tried to explain to Robin, it is precisely in anticipation of such emergencies that I am driven to carting about forty tons of luggage along every time I spend a night away from home.

Two white coated flunkeys were waiting at a respectful distance in the hall, and Kit bounded forward and shook hands with each of them, very much the young master home from the wars, and Sarah asked them if they would be so very kind as to bring our luggage in from the car. She then led the way to the drawing room, saying she felt sure we were ready for a drink. In a sense she was right because one glimpse of the room was enough to send anyone of a nervous disposition straight to the bottle. It was about fifty feet long and a cross between a baronial hall and a gothic cathedral. There were imposing stone fireplaces at opposite ends of the room, and the windows were tall narrow slits, pointed at the top. No doubt they had originally contained leaded, stained glass panes, but these had been replaced by single sheets of clear glass, which made them look even more bizarre and hideous.

In contrast to all this pseudo-mediaeval horror, the decor and furnishings were of the Beauchamp Place variety, with crystal chandeliers, Regency sofas and console tables dotted around all over the place. I cannot imagine how the problem of filling such a room would have best been tackled, but certainly the Benson-Jones answer left much to be desired.

Seeing my blank expression, Sarah laughed and linked her arm in mine.

'Yes, isn't it a monster? I hope Kit warned you, but the trouble is that we've all become so used to it that it hardly bothers us now. It's so utterly ghastly that in some strange way one ends by becoming quite attached to it. This is Julie, by the way, my twin sister; which you get no prizes for having guessed.'

She had been almost hidden in a high backed, wing armchair when we came in but now made a clumsy attempt to rise. Kit walked over and kissed her, pushing her back in the chair, and she remained seated when Sarah and I approached, smiling up at me and stretching out her hand. I understood exactly what Kit had meant. It was when she smiled that her likeness to Sarah was most noticeable, but her face in repose fell into discontented lines, which blurred the resemblance. She had the same oval face, the same dark hair and enormous dark eyes as Sarah, but the hand which had assembled them had fumbled a little, as though growing bored on the second time around, and the vitality and sparkle had been left out completely. You could tell they were related, but they were no more identical than the fifth carbon copy is to the original page of typing.

Julie was also wearing a silk trouser suit, but in an unbecoming shade of acid green, and she sat with one foot turned inwards and tucked behind the other, which effectually drew attention to her disability instead of concealing it.

'Do please sit down,' Sarah begged me, as though her happiness depended on it, 'and tell me what you'd like to drink.'

'Gin and something, please.'

'Everything's there. Kit had better mix it for you, as he probably knows how you like it. And help yourself at the same time, darling. Or would it be more sensible to take it upstairs with you?' she went on turning back to me. 'Then I could show you your room. Perhaps that might be best? Which would you honestly prefer?'

'Whatever you say,' I replied, puzzled by so much fuss over a seemingly trivial question, for she was frowning with as much gravity as if the outcome would affect us both for the rest of our lives.

'Yes, I think that might be best, you know. It will give you more time to change and you must be dying for a bath. Not that there's the least hurry because dinner won't be ready for another hour; and it's only ourselves, and Magnus of course. Come along and I'll show you the way. You're in your usual room, Kit, next door to Julie and me.'

It was not a long speech, but contained enough puzzles to keep me occupied for a week, and I maintained a pensive silence as she led me back to the hall and up one of the pair of stone staircases, which curved round to meet in a balustraded gallery on the first landing. Sarah was obliging enough to unravel one small mystery for me when we arrived there. Pointing out her bedroom, she said:

'Julie and I share one, we always did as small children, and we went back to it again when she was ill and needed so much attention. Somehow or other it's become a fixture now. It probably strikes you as rather odd, at our age, but our room is about the size of the ballroom at Versailles, so it's not quite so claustrophobic as it sounds. This one is yours, and I do hope you'll be comfortable. Don't be put off by the bed, incidentally; the mattress belongs to this century,' she added, bouncing up and down on it to demonstrate the point.

It was a black oak four poster with a carved wooden canopy and would have looked more at home in a museum, and the other furnishings were cast in the same sombre mould. Personally, I found the effect uninspiring but curiously restful after the crazy juxtaposition of periods in the drawing room. Reading my thoughts again, or perhaps merely proving that they followed a well beaten track, Sarah remarked:

'Most of the bedroom furniture was thrown in with the house, so we decided not to change it. We had to start from scratch in the downstairs rooms and Magnus utterly refused to be parted from his beloved treasures. I'm afraid that hideous neo-Gothic isn't the most suitable setting for them, poor dears, but one does see his point. Things get so ruined when they go into store, and we keep hoping that the right sort of house will come on the market.'

'So you haven't always lived here?'

'Oh heavens, no; only two years.'

My suitcases had been brought up, but not unpacked and I began on the one which did not contain the evening trouser suit. The wardrobe was lined with the same fleur de lys

pattern as the walls and contained about fifty quilted coat
hangers covered in matching silk. Sarah remained seated
on the bed and, concluding that she was in the mood for a
chat, I gave her another cue:

'What made you move here then, if you think it's so
awful?'

'Politics,' she replied cryptically, pausing while I dutifully
registered surprise, and then adding: 'Magnus is standing
for parliament at the next general election. We used to live
in Gloucestershire but as soon as he was adopted here he
decided it would be a smart move to buy a house in his own
constituency.'

'He must be pretty confident of getting in. Is it one of
those safe seats?'

'The answer to that is yes and no. He's confident all right,
but it's not a safe seat in the sense you probably mean. In
fact it's been a Tory stronghold for generations whereas
Magnus is Labour.'

This time I evinced as much astonishment as I felt certain
was expected of me.

'How very impressive!'

'His being a Socialist?'

'Not so much that. Lots of people are, but I never heard
of one investing in a mansion on this scale on such a slim
chance of its turning out to be their own constituency. It's
what I call optimistic.'

'Well, Magnus is an optimist, although "positive thinking"
is the way he describes it, and things invariably do work out
exactly as he's planned them. Besides, if you think of it in a
practical way, coming to live here makes a lot of sense. The
voters are far more likely to take him to their hearts if he's
involved in local affairs, boosting up trade and so on, than
if he were some impersonal figure who appeared on the

scene to hold a public meeting once in a while. And you'd be surprised, Tessa, what a lot of petty snobbery still exists in these rural areas. There are plenty of die-hard Tories around, who believe Magnus wants to take all their money away and nationalise the public schools, but most of them are tickled pink to be invited here.'

'Yes, I can imagine; but what does he get out of it? More power?'

'Oh no, that's quite a minor incentive. This is a cause he's really dedicated to, almost a crusade. It was why he was so dead keen on getting adopted here. It was a real challenge because the present member is the most ghastly old reactionary who ever lived. He'd like to bring back the birch and have all the immigrants sterilised, among other charming programmes, and Magnus means to see him off or bust. But I mustn't spoil it for him because he'll adore telling you all about it himself. Besides, you want to have a bath and I'm holding you up. Come down when you're ready. There's absolutely no hurry.'

It was not the first time she had reminded me I wanted a bath and perhaps she had some excuse, for I had removed my make-up in a hurry and the forty mile drive had doubtless added its quota of scruffiness. Nevertheless I suspected there was more to it than this. Although I had placed Sarah as a fairly patronising, father-fixated old gasbag, at the same time I doubted whether she often spoke at random, and in hinting that I should take time and trouble over my appearance it was possible that she wished me to make a favourable impression on her father. If so, her reasoning was quite beyond me but at least there was no conflict of aims, and I went downstairs looking as daisy petal fresh as half an hour's concentrated work could achieve.

CHAPTER THREE

1

THERE must be numerous reasons for children calling parents by their Christian names, but to assess the individual case correctly you have to know which side initiated the custom. So far as the Benson-Jones family was concerned, it had probably come about by mutual consent, for I cannot think of any man who projected a fainter Daddy-image than Sir Magnus, nor one who would have more disliked being labelled with it. Had I been asked to guess, I should have placed him in his early fifties, not so much on account of his youthful buoyancy as for the fact that he never used his seniority as a privilege and I never heard him quote his own longer experience to gain a point.

Apart from his grey-green eyes, enormously magnified by thick lensed glasses and reminding me faintly of oysters, he was an undistinguished looking man, powerful and stocky, with a flattish face and spreading nose; but it was easy to see where Sarah had got her vitality and drive. Virile and dynamic were the words I mentally applied to Sir Magnus and I feel sure he would have approved of my choice, for I never met anyone who so conspicuously paraded these qualities.

They can be attractive in well rationed doses but are apt to become wearing when unrestricted, and Sir Magnus had not eliminated this fault. During the first half of dinner he talked to me almost exclusively about his theories for re-organising the film industry, of whose economics he plainly knew a great deal more than I did, and during the second half gave me a detailed account of a discussion he had had with the Home Secretary relating to a shake up in the Police Force. A certain amount of bombast and name dropping went into this, but the implication was always present that my own views were at least of equal importance; and, curiously enough, many of the reforms which he listed would have had Robin's full endorsement. Nevertheless, I found the tirade, and the alertness it required of me, somewhat exhausting at the end of a difficult day.

He rarely spoke to Julie on his other side, except occasionally to ask her if she was enjoying herself, a question which also came my way from time to time; but he frequently called down the table to enlist Sarah's comments on some point or other, and she always responded with admirable poise and promptness. It was, needless to say, a refectory table which in its day had probably accommodated about sixty monks at each sitting, so they were obliged to conduct these exchanges in raised voices, and yet I had the impression that it was not really necessary for them to do so. Even when talking or, more rarely, listening to Kit, I sensed that Sarah had one ear permanently cocked to catch her father's every word and that she could guess by some special tone or inflexion exactly when she would be called upon to intervene. It was as though they were both playing some elaborate game, of which only they knew the rules. In view of the meagreness and apathy of their audience, I could not think why they should bother, but it may have been sheer force of habit.

'All forced of course,' Sir Magnus announced at this point in my reflections, causing the spoon I was holding to clatter against the dish. The dessert was being handed round and I was helping myself from a huge bowl of glistening strawberries.

'Under cloches, you know,' he explained. 'Not bad, is it, for early April? Sarah, you'll have to remind Cathcart not to pick any tomorrow. We want to save as many as we can for

Saturday. For the fête, you know,' he explained, lowering his voice again as he turned back to me. 'Strawberry teas. How much do you suppose we could sting 'em for that? Twenty-five? Fifty?'

'Wouldn't it rather depend on how many strawberries they got?' I suggested.

'Would it? I hadn't thought of it in that way. You may be right but my idea was that people would be attracted by the rarity element. Something to brag about to their friends. When they're in that frame of mind they don't usually stop to ask themselves whether they're getting value for money, do you think? Do you play bridge, by the way?'

'Not for money.'

'Is that so? You're not a gambler? Well, I believe in being cautious, up to a point. The trick is to know when to break out and act boldly. Do you agree?'

'Yes, and I'm sure it's one you've mastered.'

'To some extent,' he admitted, 'but perhaps not so successfully as I like to think. My worst mistakes have come from being over-cautious, counting the strawberries as it were. And I'm not just talking about money, you understand?'

'I shall try to remember your advice,' I told him.

'Yes, but you shouldn't necessarily act on it, you know. Much better if we all follow our own star and go along at our own rate. Enjoying yourself, are you?'

"Very much, thank you.'

'Yes, I can see you are. Well, we've got some nice neighbours coming in after dinner. You'll be interested to meet them. That's why I asked if you liked bridge. Babs is a first class player. But it doesn't matter if you're not keen. We can play something else. What shall it be, Julie? Any ideas?'

'Oh no, I mean, anything you like,' she replied in a fluster. 'Why not let Tessa choose?'

Since my social accomplishments in this field do not include anything more sophisticated than demon patience, I was rather unnerved by this proposal, but Sarah weighed in just in time with my reprieve.

I could almost have sworn that something had now been said which she had not been prepared for. Her tone remained casual, but she had abandoned the pretence of being immersed in her conversation with Kit. Speaking directly to her father, she called up the table:

'Don't be such a tease, Magnus! You know very well that Julie is far too unselfish to want to choose for all of us. And perhaps Tessa hates party games? Have you asked her? I was thinking we might have some music this evening.'

'Well no, that wouldn't do, would it?' he replied equably. 'The Grahams are coming, aren't they, and we all know how Babs feels about music.'

'Which reminds me,' Sarah said briskly, 'we shall have to give them coffee, so Fernando had better serve it in the drawing room. We'll leave you and Kit to hammer out the programme while I go and tell him.'

Sir Magnus bounded up and pulled back my chair, whereupon Kit came out of his dream and performed the same service for Julie, though bungling it a little, so that the chair fell backwards on the floor. He set it on its feet again, reseated himself and grabbed the port decanter.

'The trouble with Magnus,' Julie confided to me as she limped along at my side to the drawing room, 'is that he's got such enormous energy that he's literally incapable of spending an evening doing nothing. He considers every minute wasted when he's not throwing himself into some activity, however frivolous. Some people find it rather trying.'

I thought she might be one of them, for she was looking strained and anxious, and to boost her up I said:

'I suppose that's the penalty of having a tycoon for a father. They're all the same, I'm told. Can't ever relax.'

'It's not so much that,' she replied, frowning and speaking as solemnly as if I had propounded an entirely new theory. 'In some ways, he spends a lot more time relaxing than most people, but he works just as hard at it as he does at everything else.'

Sarah entered the room, wearing her public face again, and every inch the imperturbable hostess.

'I hope you won't mind too much waiting for your coffee, Tessa, but I've asked them to hold it up till the others arrive.'

'Did you know he'd invited the Grahams tonight?' Julie asked her.

'Umm. I'd forgotten, as a matter of fact. Perhaps he did mention it, or perhaps he didn't see any need to.'

'More practical to mention it when he hasn't invited them.'

'True.'

They were conversing in a clipped, offhand way, very much, I imagined, as they did when there were no outsiders around and to remind them of the presence of one I said:

'Tell me about the Grahams.'

'Magnus should do that,' Sarah answered, as her father came bounding into the room, followed at a more wavering pace by Kit. 'They're his protégés. At least, Martin is. Tell Tessa about Martin, Magnus.'

'Not heard of him? No, there's no reason why you should. Are you interested in ceramics?'

'Not to the point of hysteria. Is that what he does?'

'Among other things. He's got a pottery about four or five miles from here. Village called Missendale. Makes quite a good thing out of it too. At least he does now. He was in rather a poor way when we first came here. Brilliant chap, you know, but not enough capital, that was the whole trouble.'

'But you've straightened it out for him?'

'Oh well, we managed to fix him up with some of the modern equipment, electric kiln and all that kind of thing. And I was fortunate enough to have a little pull with a few outlets in London. Most of his stuff goes up there nowadays, but we've got a local exhibition coming up in a week or two, and there'll be some of his stuff on display at our do on Saturday. Most important to encourage these regional crafts, you know.'

'It's stretching it a bit to call it a regional craft,' Julie protested mildly. 'He could do it just as well in Scotland or the south of France.'

'Nevertheless, he has chosen to do it here.'

'Only because he had to move somewhere and this place was going cheap and near enough to London to suit Babs.'

'He used to live in Sussex,' Sarah explained. 'Babs was married to the local doctor but she left him and ran off with Martin. This is not just scandal-mongering. It's much better that you should know about it and spare yourself some possible gaffes. But Julie is quite right, of course.'

'Well, all that's in the past now,' Magnus said firmly, but without a trace of annoyance. 'The point is that if you haven't got any indigenous craftsmen, the next best thing is to adopt some. I see nothing against that. In the end, it creates a certain pride, not to mention employment, among the local people and the skills get handed on to them.'

'Except that most of Martin's trainees come from overseas,' Julie remarked. 'So the skills actually get handed on to Nigeria and Australia.'

'That's perfectly true,' he agreed. 'But it also has certain built-in advantages, don't you think? A small influx of foreigners in our midst must help to break down these odious racial prejudices. Surely we should be grateful for that alone?'

I believe Julie had been ready to continue the discussion, but Magnus abruptly turned away from her, saying:

'Well now, Kit! You haven't much to say for yourself. Do we bore you?'

Presumably he had been hitting the bottle harder than I had realised, for he opened his eyes, said: 'Oh, definitely, sir,' and immediately closed them again.

Julie let out a nervous squeak and even Magnus looked faintly nonplussed. Sarah said impatiently: 'Wake up, Kit, for goodness sake!' exactly as though he were a child misbehaving himself.

Kit opened his eyes again and blearily focused them on her.

'Whassat? Oh, sorry! Fact is, it's been quite a day. Going to bed now. No games for Christopher tonight.'

Holding on tightly to the arms of his chair and fumbling his feet a little, in a series of uncharacteristically clumsy movements, he managed to stand up. He was sweating a bit too, and it was partly an instinctive impulse to help him make a dignified exit, partly opportunism which caused me to get to my feet as well.

'Nor for me, either. Kit's right, we're both rather jaded. If you won't think it rude, I'll . . .'

As I spoke, the door opened and four people entered the room, followed by the butler bearing a silver tray of coffee and liqueurs. Without a tremor, Sarah rose to greet them. In doing so, she had to pass close to Kit and, without glancing at him, she stuck out her right hand and jabbed him in the chest. It may have been intended as a playful gesture, but evidently there was some force behind it, for Kit collapsed in his chair like a sack of coals, a comical expression of disbelief on his face as, with teeth aflash, Sarah continued on her way to welcome the visitors.

2

The procession was headed by Babs Graham, the only woman of the party, and she advanced upon us with both arms outstretched, all eager smiles and jangling bracelets. She rivalled Sarah in vivacity, but in no other respect, being quite ten years older and at the same time much more youthfully dressed. She also had coarser features, far too much blue eye shadow and an over-effusive manner. Nevertheless, I could understand some people finding her attractive.

She was followed by her husband, a slight, bearded man with hungry, mad looking eyes, which he fixed on me with an unnerving stare while he wrung my hand, as though inviting me to break down and confess my sins on the spot.

The other two were both much younger. One was a gangling, red headed youth, with a loping walk and an over-developed Adam's apple, and I was told that his name was Walter Greig and that he came from South Africa. He spoke in a twangy voice, sounding his 'r's' as though he were grinding them out with a pestle and mortar. Last of all and hanging back a bit, perhaps from laziness rather than shyness, came Henry Ngali Mbwala. I confess that I did not grasp this with perfect accuracy at the time, but I was subsequently to see his name in print far too often to forget it now.

He must have been about the same age as Walter, not more than twenty, and presumably they shared a common interest in pots, but there the resemblance ended. If the passionate and proselytising glint in Martin's eyes denoted, as had been hinted, a keen desire for racial integration, he had certainly plunged in at the deep end with this pair.

Henry was small and compact, with slender hands and feet. What chiefly set him apart from the herd, however, was his way of speaking English. It was a more melodious brand than Walter's, but a lot harder to understand, for he had a trick of accentuating all the syllables which are normally swallowed, and of rounding off his sentences with high pitched peals of laughter. It was puzzling at first, but I eventually reached the conclusion that he had learnt English from books, long before hearing it spoken and that the laughter was set off by the bewilderment on the faces of everyone around him.

Pausing only to embrace Sarah and say how much she had to tell her, Babs pursued a straight course to Magnus and, watching her go to work on him, I began to understand Sarah's motives for grooming me into a counter-attraction for her father. Whether or not she had known the Grahams had been invited was probably immaterial. Magnus was clearly in a fair way to becoming besotted by Babs, and from Sarah's point of view, no potential diversion was too hopeless to be neglected. However, I was only prepared to play her game up to a certain limit, and did not wait meekly for Magnus to remember my existence and ask me if I was enjoying myself. I left him to it and took my coffee cup over to the tray, where Sarah was in charge.

'What kind of music do you like?' I asked her. 'Not pop, I imagine?'

'Oh, sometimes. All sorts, really. Nothing highbrow, I assure you.'

'Do you play yourself?'

'Yes, we all do. In a very amateurish way, I hasten to add. Mainly for our own amusement, you know, although Julie stands in for our church organist occasionally.'

'All this and talent too!' I remarked sadly. 'It's not fair.'

'No, it's not,' she agreed. 'But don't misunderstand me. It's not that we have more talent than other people; less probably, although my mother was very musical. It's simply that we've had unlimited opportunity to develop our potential. Do you realise that nine tenths of the population go to their graves without even discovering what they're capable of? That's where the true inequality lies, and it's the kind of thing which Magnus is fighting.'

'Rather an ambitious programme, I should have thought.'

'Maybe, but it makes practical sense too. It's not just a Utopian dream. Imagine trying to run a factory with only one tenth of the plant in working order! And yet that's precisely how most of the world is run, under our present system.'

Conceivably she was right, but I wished she would step down from her soap box once in a while, and also stop quoting her father every time she opened her mouth. I did not consider that either of these traits boded well for her marriage, and with this in mind I said:

'I suppose you'll miss it all?'

'All what?'

'Taking such a big part in your father's campaign. I expect you'll be sorry to give it up, in some ways?'

'But, Tessa, I have no intention of giving it up.'

'Oh, really?'

'Why on earth should I? Kit will have his job and I shall carry on with mine. There's nothing unusual in that. Lots of women combine marriage with a career, as you should know.'

'Yes, but it's not all plain sailing, and besides your circumstances are slightly different.'

'In what way?'

'Well, for instance, I'm sure you know all about this marvellous offer Kit's had from America? If he takes it, and he'd be a fool not to, it could mean his staying over there for six months or even longer. You could hardly do your canvassing from New York or Hollywood.'

'No, of course not, but the problem doesn't arise. I haven't the faintest intention of going to New York or Hollywood.'

'You'd let Kit go on his own? That's not exactly what I'd describe as combining a career with marriage. In fact, I doubt if by the end of it there would be any marriage left to combine.'

'I entirely agree, and it's one reason why I'm against his going. I think he'd be insane while there's still plenty of work for him in this country.'

'In other words, your career is more important than his?'

'Oh dear me no, not at all. I hope I'm not as selfish and arrogant as that. I wouldn't dream of standing in his way if I truly believed the American job would be good for him; but you see, Tessa, I don't. Not at this stage, anyway, when he still lacks experience. America can be a pretty tough place, you know, and the only way to shine there is to have something to offer which no one else has got.'

There was a good deal of truth in this, but I was not sure that it applied in Kit's case, or even that she had bothered to consider whether it did or not. However, it was really none of my business and, presumably mistaking my silence for agreement, she moved closer and said in even more earnest and confidential tones:

'In fact, Tessa, you'd be a real friend if you'd put in a word to dissuade him. He admires you tremendously, as a fellow actor I mean, and he'd listen to you. I wouldn't ask this if I didn't honestly believe that it was in his own best interests, but I do. I'd like you to believe that.'

I did not doubt it for a second, and the strangely naive thing about Sarah was her sublime confidence that she had only to express the wish that I should believe something and it was as good as done. I saw no point in disillusioning her, however, and fortunately a loud cackle of amusement from her father had now diverted her attention. There was no telling what had provoked his merriment, but Babs was sharing it to the full. They were laughing together on the sofa like a couple of school children, and I could see by the narrowing of her eyes that Sarah's thoughts were now focused on more pressing problems than Kit's career. I watched with interest as she went into action, tilting her head and stretching her mouth into the electric smile as she strolled towards them like some beautiful tigress loosening up for the spring.

'Want some more coffee?' I asked, perching on the arm of Kit's chair.

'No, all I want is to take my tiny self up to beddy byes.'

'Me too. Why don't we take them by surprise and make a dash for it?'

'Trouble is, at this precise moment of time, dashing is rather out. I am very slightly paralytic.'

'Perhaps some fresh air would help? Come on! Hang on to me and we'll act like we're going for a chummy stroll in the garden.'

'Do you mind? It's pitch bloody dark.'

'I know, but we don't really have to walk and the air might pull you round.'

He blinked at me, as though considering the proposal in a fuddled way, then slowly nodded his head. 'You may have something there,' he informed me with great solemnity.

He managed to stand upright without falling flat on his face and, keeping myself between him and the others, I propelled him over to the central window and turned the iron ring handle which opened the whole pane outwards on to the garden. The only remaining obstacle was the sill, which was about a foot above the floor, but Kit was bearing up moderately well and I had high hopes of his negotiating this without attracting unwelcome attention. They were doomed, however, for the operation was only half completed when Sarah called out in bright, governessy tones:

'Come along, everyone! We're going to play musical consequences. It's just the same as the ordinary kind but you're only allowed to use characters and titles from opera.'

It was all Kit needed and giving the window a violent push he blundered over the sill and disappeared into the night. This brought Sarah to my side in a flash.

'What's the matter? Where's Kit gone?'

'I should leave him to it,' I advised her. 'The last Cointreau may have been a drop too much. We thought the air might freshen him up a bit.'

'You mean he's drunk?' she enquired incredulously.

'Not to beat about the bush, yes.'

'Oh, heavens! Well, I suppose you're right. We'd better leave him to sober up. Or should I go and see?' she asked, glancing back over her shoulder at Magnus and Babs, once more in intimate conversation on the sofa.

'I'll go, if you like, Sarah. Just make sure he hasn't fallen in the swimming pool or something. If I were you, I'd start the game without us. We'd be hopeless at it, anyway.'

'That's awfully kind of you, Tessa. I would be most grateful. Magnus gets so cruelly bored with small talk, and it might be better if I keep him amused until Kit's pulled himself together. He doesn't terribly approve of that kind of behaviour.'

*

His last small spurt had apparently exhausted Kit, for he had moved only a few yards from the window and was leaning against a tree.

'How's it going?' I asked him.

'Never worse. This was a lousy idea. Go inside, for God's sake. I think I'm going to be sick.'

Whereupon he plunged away from me towards a clump of bushes and disappeared from view.

I waited to see if he would return, less from concern for his welfare than the passionate desire to miss at least one round of the ghastly game, but five minutes went by without a sign of him. Since it was a cold as well as boring vigil, I gave in and climbed back through the window, shutting it behind me but leaving the curtains drawn to light the way for Kit if he ever returned.

With the exception of Henry, who was wisely recharging his batteries with a comfortable snooze, they were all sitting round, industriously scribbling away with their little pencils and pads, and I awarded Sarah full marks for generalship. Babs was now decorously paired off with her husband, Julie sat with Magnus and Sarah beside Walter, apparently quite content to fill in his contributions as well as her own. Rather ludicrous they all looked too, in my opinion, frowning and tapping their teeth with the pencils and pulling rueful little grimaces as they passed the slips of paper round and round.

'Ready to join in now?' Magnus asked me when the results had been read out amidst rather misplaced hilarity.

'No, I think I'd rather be a spectator. You've already used up the only titles I know.'

'Then let's play something else. What's it to be, Sarah? Think of something that Tessa would enjoy. We can't leave her out, you know. I'll give you a drink, Tessa, while they're all making up their minds.'

He walked over to the tray and, searching desperately for a means of escape, I said:

'No, really, thank you, I won't have any more. In fact, if you don't mind, I—'

I paused in mid-stream; the silence was broken by a crash of glass behind me, and a flying object went skimming over my head. Concluding that the I.R.A. had arrived, I pitched sideways and fell on my knees, burying my head in the nearest armchair and covering it with a cushion. The expected explosion did not follow, although I heard muffled squeals and shouts. Someone moved swiftly past me, there were more sounds of shattering glass, and when I nerved myself to break cover I found that everyone had moved around a bit. Magnus was now in the middle of the room, also on his knees, although it was obviously not cowardice which had driven him there. He looked as composed as any man could in that position, but Sarah was bending over him, examining a cut on his left temple, which he was mopping at with a handkerchief.

On the carpet about two feet away from him there was a fair sized brick, with a piece of paper still partially attached to it by rubber bands. I moved forward for a closer look, but Magnus was ahead of me. He made a grab for the brick and wrenched the paper free.

'I don't think you ought to do that,' I told him, all my training coming to the fore. 'There might be fingerprints.' It would be gratifying to record that he instantly drew back his hand in the manner of one bitten by a serpent, and indeed I did perceive a fractional hesitation, but only sufficient for Sarah to swoop on the paper instead. She took it over to a table lamp and slowly and deliberately smoothed out the folded sheet.

I turned to Julie. 'Oughtn't you to ring the police? They might be in time to catch whoever did it while he's still in the grounds.'

'Oh no,' she replied nervously, her eyes on Sarah. 'I don't think we'd want the police brought in. It was probably only some silly boys from the village trying to scare us. Besides, Walter's already gone after them.'

'Oh, was that Walter who went out? How brave of him! Do you suppose he's all right? If there are several of them they may be giving him a rough time.'

'No, Walter can take care of himself. He may look rather weedy, but he played Rugby for his university or something, so he won't have much trouble dealing with a bunch of yobs. The only thing that worries me is . . .' She broke off, biting her lip, as Sarah handed the grubby piece of paper to her father. He had moved into a chair by this time, still holding the bloodstained handkerchief to his head:

'I can't read it without my glasses,' he complained fretfully. 'They're down there on the floor somewhere.'

'Not to worry,' Sarah said in a nursie voice. 'It's not important, just stupid hooliganism. What we ought to do is to put some disinfectant on that cut and see if it needs stitching. Come along upstairs and I'll bathe it for you.'

'No, read this out first.'

'Aloud?'

'Otherwise I shan't hear, shall I? There's no need to be squeamish. The others were all here when it happened, and they have a right to know what it says. Luckily, it happened to be I who was struck but it could just as well have been one of them.'

'All the same, I don't think this is quite the moment for a post mortem,' Sarah told him. 'I think we should see to that cut before anything else.'

While saying this, she had shaken her head very slightly and glanced obliquely at Henry. The rumpus had woken him up but he looked noticeably cooler than the rest of us, which made Sarah's warning gestures rather a puzzle. Their significance was evidently not lost on Magnus, however, for he capitulated at once. Standing up, he crumpled the piece of paper in his hand and aimed it at the fireplace. It fell short and landed on the hearthrug and at this point the final scene in the evening's entertainment got off to a resounding start.

The door was flung open and two figures came lurching through. One of them was Walter, and he was supporting Kit, who appeared to be semi-conscious. With a wild moan of distress, Julie went limping down the room towards them and seized Kit's hand.

'Oh, what's happened? Are you all right, Kit? Oh look, my God, you're hurt!'

He did not answer and together she and Walter lugged him on to a chair, where he sank back with a feeble groan.

'It was my fault, I guess,' Walter explained, scarlet with embarrassment, 'but I didn't know who he was, see? Came on him out in the garden and took him for the culprit. It was only after I'd punched him on the nose that I realised. The other fellow must have got away. Too bad I had to go after the wrong man.'

'Not altogether,' Magnus told him. 'You seem to have been a little hasty, but Kit's injuries don't look too serious, and we might have been in real trouble if you'd beaten up one of the local chaps. Well, Babs, my dear, and Martin, I must apologise to you both for this somewhat unhappy evening. I don't imagine any of us wishes to prolong it. I shall say goodnight now, and wish you all a safe journey home. If Walter has brought his bike, he can be your outrider and you need have no fears with such protection as that. I think the least said about this business the better, and I feel sure I can rely on your discretion.'

At the end of this little admonitory speech, they all moved out to the hall, leaving the room to me and a comatose Kit, and I seized the chance to indulge my curiosity on another subject. I quickly stooped down and retrieved the crumpled piece of paper, read through the brief message and then tossed it down again. It was written in red crayon and capital letters, and ran as follows:

'YOU ARE A TRAITOR AND WE ARE WATCHING YOU SEND THE BLACKIES HOME WHERE THEY BELONG WE DONT WANT THEM HERE THIS IS YOUR FINAL WARNING FROM THE CLEAN UP BRITAIN CRUSADE'.

CHAPTER FOUR

1

'GOOD morning, Miss Julie,' I said, flopping down on the grass beside her. 'How are the invalids today?'

I had breakfasted in my room and foreseeing only limited scope for enjoyment in the hours ahead, had delayed my descent until past ten o'clock. I could just as well have dragged it out still further because there was no one about when I came downstairs and I had eventually wandered out to the garden where two marquees had already been set up on the lawn. The first one was empty but in the second I had come upon Julie, crouched on her hands and knees and fussing about with some tubs of potted tulips and forget-menots, which were placed around each of the posts supporting the striped canopy roof.

'Kit's much better,' she replied. 'He came down for break-fast. But please don't call me that.'

'And your father?'

'Recovering rapidly, so Sarah tells me. Did you sleep well?'

'Yes, thank you, but why mustn't I call you Miss Julie?'

'Oh, such a pathetic, contemptible creature,' she replied, sitting back on her heels and then flopping sideways as they gave way under her. 'And the horrid thing is that I some-times feel I'm exactly like her.'

'It's a good play,' I remarked. 'The trouble is that to make her behaviour credible the odious Jean has to possess enormous physical magnetism, and not many actors have it. Offhand I can only think of two and they're both in their sixties. What's this tent going to be used for?'

'The flower and vegetable display. They'll be bringing the tables in this morning, and I want to make sure they don't damage these plants.'

'All this is going to make rather a hash of your lawn, isn't it?'

'It doesn't matter. Magnus is quite prepared to have it returfed if necessary. Perhaps Kit could do it? How about that?'

'I hardly think so,' I replied, wondering if she were off her head. 'I wouldn't have said gardening was quite in his line.'

She laughed. 'No, I meant that he might do for the man in Miss Julie. Or too fundamentally sympathetic perhaps?'

Unfortunately her explanation did nothing to resolve the problem, for it was now a matter of deciding whether she was so besotted with love as genuinely to believe that Kit was competent to play such a role, or so besotted with love that no excuse was too flimsy to drag in the idol's name.

'I should say Henry would be even better,' I remarked, hoping to ridicule the subject out of existence.

She had bent forward to pick a dead leaf off one of the flowers, but she looked up sharply, her face flushing as she said:

'What makes you say that?'

'One has the sense that underneath that sleepy exterior there's some of the quality I was talking about,' I replied, warming to the theme. 'I realise that Strindberg didn't mean Jean to be coloured, but I don't see why that should bother anyone. In fact, it might bring it a bit more up to date. Nobody nowadays would blink an eye if a repressed young woman had an affair with the valet, but if he was an African valet it might make a difference.'

'Magnus wouldn't agree with you,' she said, with a return to some forget-me-not pruning. 'Truly. Do you doubt me?'

'Of course not. That is, I don't doubt your sincerity. I just think you've been very slightly brainwashed. For instance, Julie, did you read that note which came flying in on the brick last night?'

'Yes, we had a conference about it when we were . . . after you and Kit had gone up. Are you saying you read it too?'

'Yes. As your father pointed out, it could have hit any one of us, me included, so naturally, I felt curious.'

'So it would appear,' she said coolly.

'And I was particularly curious to know what it contained that was too alarming to be read out to a group of grown-up people but not nearly alarming enough to notify the police.'

'And did you find out?'

'Naturally. In a flash. The reason for not reading it aloud and not informing the police was the same: to spare Henry embarrassment. Right?'

'Exactly, and doesn't it prove my point? Magnus is just as considerate of coloured people's feelings as anyone else's. Perhaps even more so.'

'Oh, definitely even more so, I should say.'

'I can't see anything shameful in that,' she retorted, staring down at a little pile of grass which she had been plucking out in handfuls.

'It probably indicates great sensitivity, but patronage is still patronage, whatever form it takes.'

I don't know whether she heard this because we were interrupted. A man walked backwards into the tent, holding up one end of a long trestle table. Both he and his opposite number wore green baize aprons and if they were not actually pulling the forelock it was probably only because to do so would have interfered with the job in hand for their attitude was redolent of solemn servility. This was no doubt for Sarah's benefit for she brought up the procession looking stern and preoccupied.

'That's right, Mr Best, along the left side, please. Now, just a little further down your end, if you wouldn't mind. Thank you very much, that's perfect. The other one is to go along the opposite side and when you bring it in please be awfully careful not to knock the flowers . . . . Oh, there you are, Julie! Are you feeling all right?'

'Fine, thanks. Why?'

'Just that it's unlike you to be lazing about when there's work to be done. Hallo, Tessa! I do hope you slept well?' Julie had already scrambled to her feet, in a series of her usual ungainly movements, and I said:

'I'm lazing about too, but you must let me know if there's anything I can do.'

'As a matter of fact, there is, if you wouldn't mind terribly. Magnus is rather keen to run through your speech for tomorrow's opening. He's prepared a rough version which I've just typed out, and what it needs now is the personal touch. One or two anecdotes or remarks of your own sprinkled around, if you can think of any.'

'Well, I might manage that, I suppose,' I said rather huffily. 'How is your father, by the way?'

'I'm not terribly happy about him, to be honest with you, Tessa. I shall be glad to have your opinion. He was quite chirpy first thing this morning, but he seems to have lapsed back. The cut is healing up beautifully, but he complains of a headache, and he hasn't eaten a thing.'

'Delayed shock?' I suggested.

'Umm, maybe; although, knowing Magnus, I don't think it's very likely. As a rule, he takes everything in his stride. He's completely fearless, for one thing. What bothers me is that there may have been some internal injury. I was going to ask you, Julie; do you think we should call in Dr Simmons? Magnus will probably be livid if we do, but we could invent some story to account for his having knocked his head and we should never forgive ourselves for neglecting it, if it turned out there was something seriously wrong. What do you think, Tessa?'

I was amused by her need, or pretence of it, for constant advice and reassurance, and suspecting that it was purely a device to obtain approval for a decision already taken, I humoured her by saying:

'I daresay it would be easier to live with his ill temper than your own remorse, so I should go ahead.'

'Yes, you're so right. How very sensible! Julie, would you be an angel . . . ? No, on second thoughts, you take Tessa up to see Magnus and I'll telephone the doctor myself. After all it is Good Friday and he may have been hoping for the day off. I shall have to put it tactfully.'

She walked with us as far as the house, musing away in silence, and presumably turning over phrases in her mind whereby to jockey the doctor into overcoming all her scruples and being the one to insist that the patient should be visited.

2

Magnus certainly did not appear to be in need of medical attention when Julie, having tapped on the door, ushered me into his bedroom which, in contrast to his colourful personality, was almost ascetic in its austerity. It had no doubt originally been a square room, but one quarter had been partitioned off to make it roughly L shaped, with the longer stroke of the L on its side and furthest away from the door. All that was visible of this part, when Julie had waved me through and then disappeared, was a plain narrow bed and some steel filing cabinets, but there was an archway into the room within the room, and as I went past I caught a glimpse of complicated gymnastic apparatus, including horizontal bars and a bicycling machine.

Magnus was sitting at his desk, which was tucked away inside the alcove formed by the partition wall, with a telephone clamped to his ear, while his right hand continued with a life of its own, methodically turning over the pages of a report. The only evidence of poor health was the bandage round his head and the fact that he was still in pyjamas and dressing gown.

On the wall facing him hung the single incongruous object in the room, a full length, life size portrait rather in the style of Sargent, of a young woman bedecked in white satin and pearls. She had fluffy blonde hair and light blue eyes, but the oval face and high domed forehead were so exactly those of Sarah and Julie that, except for the colouring, one of them could easily have posed for it.

Apart from this, the most prominent feature was the desk, which was at least as large as the bed and had two telephones on it, one red and one green. It was the green one which had been engaging part of his attention but after swivelling round to take a look at me he instructed the caller to ring him back on the same number in twenty minutes and dropped the receiver on to its hook.

'One of my colleagues has over-reached himself,' he explained. 'It's casting a gloom over his weekend and he'd like me to bob over to Munich and pull him out of the mess, but he's going to have to think of something else.'

'No, you could hardly be expected to dash about the continent in your state of health.'

'Nonsense, my dear child, there's nothing wrong with me that a couple of aspirin won't cure. It's tomorrow's gala I'm thinking of. Can't afford any hitches there, after all the work and organisation we've put into it.'

'And might there be a hitch, if you weren't there to supervise?'

'No, most unlikely, I should imagine. The real reason is that I mean to enjoy myself. And I hope that goes for you too?'

'I expect I will, once I've got through the ghastly speech.'

'Don't give it a thought. If you look half as pretty as you do now, we shan't have a thing to worry about. You could read out the train timetable and have them clamouring for more. Still, I've no doubt you'll feel more confident if you've got it all at your finger tips, aren't I right? Yes, I thought so. So what I'd like you to do is to cast your eye over this draft

I've roughed out, and then tell me of any alterations you'd like made to it, any little words or phrases which sound unnatural, if you see what I mean?'

He handed me two typewritten pages, comprising a total of half a dozen paragraphs. The first pertained to the history and growth of the South Midlands Conservation Society, the middle part carried a more personal flavour and contained, as Sarah had warned me, blank spaces for the interpolation of remarks of my own composition, and it ended with a rousing call to arms. I read it through and handed it back to him, saying:

'There's only one bit which is not at all in my style.'

'Yes? Where's that? Tell me what it is and we'll put it right.'

'Nearly at the end, in your peroration,' I said, and began to read aloud:

' . . . gathered together here, amongst all our friends, in this beautiful English countryside of ours, all of us out to spend money and enjoy ourselves, we may perhaps be excused if we forget the common aim which has brought us here. We may even wish to thrust from our minds for once the problems and dangers which surround us and threaten the survival of this same beloved countryside, along with our human right to enjoy ourselves in our own way. But I should remind you that it is only by our vigilance that we can retain these privileges for ourselves and our children and our grandchildren. There are those who seek to deprive us of them, and some of them speak to us in honeyed voices, so we must be ever on our guard; ready to oppose them with all our strength and resolution and not to falter in the struggle to preserve our glorious heritage.'

I looked up and Magnus said: 'Yes? What's the trouble? What don't you like about it?'

'Well, it's politicians' stuff,' I said, choosing the mildest of several criticisms which sprang to mind. 'Not the kind of thing I'd say in a million years.'

'Is it the sentiments or the language you object to?'

'Both, I'm afraid.'

'Dear me, what a pity! I was rather hoping to end on a stirring note. But never mind. I asked for your opinion and I shall certainly be guided by it. I'll strike that passage out and substitute something a little more colloquial, is that it?'

'Yes please.'

'It shall be done. Think no more about it. And that's your only criticism? Good! Splendid! Will you be able to get it off by heart in time for tomorrow afternoon?'

'Yes, easily.'

'I'm delighted to hear that, because I do think it will be so much more effective if you don't use notes. Let it appear completely spontaneous, as if you were really . . .'

'Enjoying myself?'

'Exactly. It's bound to be infectious, and that's the mood we want to create. Everyone enjoying themselves and spending a lot of money.'

'If you're so meticulous about all such minor matters, it's a mystery to me how you find time for your real work,' I remarked.

'Oh, but it's the details which count, don't you see? Anyone with training and reasonable intelligence can organise on a big scale. It's simply a question of knowing how to delegate. It's the details which require a touch of genius. No, no, I'm only joking, my dear. The fact is that Sarah's the brains of this enterprise but she indulges me by allowing me to pretend that I play a useful part.'

'You're going to miss her?'

'No doubt of that, but it has to be faced. I'm not such a monster as to want her to be tied to me for the rest of my life. Just so long as she marries the right man, who'll give her plenty of scope for her talents, that's all I ask.'

'And do you think Kit measures up to those requirements?'

'Oh yes,' he replied cheerfully. 'I shouldn't be at all surprised, you know. He doesn't lack ambition and with Sarah behind him he'll soon get to the top. I may even be allowed to lend a helping hand myself, from time to time. I've got a little pull here and there, when it's a question of raising finance for films.'

I was interested to discover that he did not share Sarah's own vision of the future, whereby she would continue with her present activities, incorporating Kit into them as a kind of extra hobby, and I was debating whether to refer to this when faintly and faraway I heard a telephone ringing. The instruments on the desk remained silent, but Magnus had instinctively turned his head towards the green one, and I was reminded that he was expecting a call. There was a more pressing matter than Sarah's future that I wanted to raise before it came through and, without much thought, I plunged straight into it:

'By the way, who's behind the Keep Britain Clean Crusade?'

'A bunch of thugs,' he replied irritably. 'How did you come to hear of them?'

'They sent you a message last night, remember?'

'Who told you that?'

'No one. I read it. No business to, maybe, but I was curious.'

'Quite right too. I shouldn't think much of you if you weren't. All the same, I'd be obliged if you'd keep it under your hat.'

'Okay, but you still haven't told me who they are.'

'My dear girl, you witnessed their behaviour, you read their infantile threats, what more do you need?'

'But it doesn't make sense. Here you are, working flat out on the ecology lark, and yet they call you a traitor. I thought keeping Britain clean was exactly what you were after?'

'And now, if I may say so, you're being disingenuous. You must have realised that the reference was not to the air we breathe but to the people who breathe it. The aim of this charming outfit is to rid the country of its non-Anglo-Saxon elements; the good old racial purity theme cropping up again with all its usual violence and prejudice.'

'And it's serious, is it? They aren't just hooligans, as you pretended?'

'Who knows how serious it is? All these crackpot campaigns which feed on fear and ignorance are potentially dangerous. It depends who's running them and what their real objective is. In this case the organisers have been careful to keep in the background. We may have our own ideas on the subject but we don't know for certain who they are or how much power they wield.'

'Has this kind of thing ever happened before?'

'No, certainly not, quite an innovation. There have been one or two anonymous letters but last night's episode was the first of its kind. An isolated incident, I feel sure, so there's no need for you to . . .'

There was a knock on the door and a few seconds later Julie came into the alcove.

'Sorry to interrupt you, Magnus, but Babs was on the telephone. First of all she wanted to know how you were.'

'How very sweet of her! I hope you told her there were no ill effects whatever?'

'More or less. She also wanted to know if we'd care to go over there this morning and look round the Pottery. She thought Tessa and Kit might be interested.'

'Splendid idea! Excellent! You'd enjoy that, wouldn't you Tessa? Tell her we accept with pleasure. Let's see now, I've got this call coming from Germany, but it shouldn't be long. Say we'll be there by twelve.'

Julie, however, continued to hover uncertainly and he said with a shade of impatience:

'Well, run along, my dear. You can't keep Babs waiting for ever.'

'No, that's all right, I've arranged to ring her back after I've consulted you all, but the point is that Sarah doesn't think you should go out today.'

'Why ever not?'

'Because of your head.'

'Oh, piffle! I certainly don't intend to skulk indoors on that account. Besides it would be most unwise. The rumour would be all round the place in no time that I was seriously injured, and that's the last thing we want, surely?'

I was fascinated by this somewhat regal attitude to the situation, as though he were no ordinary citizen but a head of state, with a duty to show himself to the multitude and scotch the rumours of assassination. Absurd though it was, I hardly doubted that Sarah would view the matter in the same light once it was pointed out to her; though, as it happened, I had overlooked an even more powerful consideration. However desirable to allay the fears of the populace and bring discomfort to the enemy, it transpired that even these noble sentiments took second place to her determination to nip Babs' little schemes in the bud. She announced with a firmness which admitted no argument that she had prevailed on Dr Simmons to call at midday and that for Magnus to be out when he arrived would create the most serious ill feeling. Sir Magnus capitulated, and twenty minutes later the party set off to Missendale without him.

After a brief consultation between the sisters Sarah took the wheel of the Bentley, with Kit beside her, and they sped off immediately. There followed some prolonged and perfectly unnecessary limping around from one side to the other on Julie's part, before she and I were installed in a natty black Jaguar, which was also parked in the drive, and took our place in the procession to the Potteries.

CHAPTER FIVE

1

THE route to Missendale took us about six miles to the north west by way of a lane which branched off from the main road beside the *Eglinton Arms*, where Kit and I had stopped on the previous evening. Julie explained to me that there was a short cut through the fields from this point, but it was only a bridle way and not wide enough for cars.

'It makes a pleasant walk, though, so they tell me. I have to take their word for it,' she added wryly.

Although the lane was narrow and winding, she took it at ferocious speed, at the same time displaying the skill and timing of the true expert, which does so much to inspire confidence in even the shakiest of passengers. I felt suffi-ciently relaxed to compliment her on her prowess.

'Thank you,' she replied, smiling secretively, and I guessed that part of her satisfaction came from the fact that driving was one of the few activities in which her lameness was no handicap. Had it not been for that, she might have been as brilliant as Sarah in other departments, and perhaps equally bossy too, which in my view went a long way towards compensating for her disability. It prompted me to say:

'This is probably an impertinence, but I think you make too much of it.'

'Too much of what?' she asked with a bafflement which sounded faintly overdone.

'Your lameness. You sometimes give the impression that you go out of your way to draw attention to it. If you don't mind my saying so, I think you should try and forget it, and then everyone else would too.'

'Oh no, they wouldn't,' she replied. 'That would never be allowed.'

It was an odd way of putting it and she did not enlighten me further, but at least I had now begun to understand her motive for the delayed start. We had swept majestically round a bend in the lane and fifty yards ahead of us, beside a cluster of ramshackle buildings standing back from the road, the Bentley had just stopped. She had given Sarah three minutes' start and even so she had caught her up.

Babs must have been lurking behind the blue repp curtains, for she emerged from the main building before a car door was opened. She looked more presentable in slacks and pullover than in her evening finery, but the veneer of affability got a few cracks in it when, having drawn a blank first at one car and then the next, she realised who was missing.

'Oh yes he's fine, thank you Babs,' Sarah said, responding to the anxious enquiries. 'Absolutely recovered, in fact, but he asked to be excused. You know how it is? So many urgent things cropping up all the time.'

That was her version for Babs. To me, having laid her well groomed hand on my arm, as the others went into the house she murmured hurriedly:

'Listen, Tessa, would you mind awfully if I were to slip away when the conducted tour sets off? One doesn't want the whole world to know, but the truth is that I am the tiniest bit worried about Magnus.'

'I don't mind in the least, but there didn't strike me as being much wrong with him.'

'Oh, really? I'm relieved to hear that because I value your opinion. All the same, you don't know Magnus quite as I do. He's quite capable of putting on an act for your benefit. Partly out of vanity, I have to admit, but mainly because he does so want you to enjoy the weekend. Also, to be perfectly frank with you, he gets so bored when he's left on his own. So, if you're quite sure you'll be all right with Julie and Kit, I'll just nip back and keep an eye on him.'

It was difficult to see why she had come at all, unless it were purely for the pleasure of witnessing Babs' disappointment. It was hard to believe her capable of such pettiness, and yet her departure was not conducted quite so unobtrusively as I had been led to expect.

'Goodbye all,' she announced gaily, having walked as far as the sitting room with me. 'Now that I've delivered my cargo I'm afraid I must dash. There's still loads to do before tomorrow. I'll take the Jag, if that's all right with you Julie? And mind you don't overtire yourself. If I were you, I'd put my feet up and let Tessa and Kit go round on their own. Thanks a lot, Babs. Come as early as you can tomorrow and don't forget to cross my palm with silver.'

'What did she mean by that?' I asked Julie, as we followed Martin into one of the outbuildings, where Henry was sitting cross legged on the floor behind a potter's wheel. She had not taken Sarah's advice literally, but at least she was clinging to Kit's arm for support, which may have been intended as a compromise. 'Can Sarah tell fortunes, among all her other talents?'

'She's going to tomorrow. Madame Rosetta, the gypsy palmist. She'll be one of the star attractions.'

'Just for a lark, or is it genuine?'

'Curiously enough, she has been known to have second sight once or twice. It started when we were children. We used to do a mind reading stunt to amuse the grown ups. It was all a trick, you know, but Magnus loved it and he encouraged us. In the end we became quite professional and Sarah occasionally pulled off something we hadn't rehearsed at all. It's odd,' she added thoughtfully, 'how a false reputation for being good at something can often end by making you genuinely good at it.'

'Sometimes,' I agreed, thinking it was a pity that this had not yet happened to Kit.

'Do you want to have a try to DO this?' Henry asked, looking up at me with his lazy, melancholy expression.

'No thanks, I'd much rather watch you.'

'Oh, go on, Tessa, have a shot! It's great fun,' Julie urged me, and I obediently squatted down beside Henry. He took a lump of clay, rolled it between his immaculate hands and then placed it on the wheel, explaining the principles to me as he went along. It must have been more fun to do than to watch, however, for no sooner had I got the thing spinning away, with predictably chaotic results, than Julie tugged at Kit's arm and led him away to inspect the new electric kiln.

'There is nothing to see there,' Henry remarked, watching them go. 'Today is GOOD Friday, a holy day, so no one is working except me,' he added with a burst of laughter.

'Perhaps you're not a Christian?'

'Oh yes,' he replied, 'Sometimes I am.'

'Not today, though?'

'MRS Graham asked me to be here. To put ON a show for the visitors.'

There was no way of telling whether these strange emphases reflected or distorted his meaning but he was so unlike anyone I had ever met that curiosity made me persevere.

'Do you mean to have a pottery of your own when you go home?'

'Yes. Or MAYBE I shall go into politics, as my father WOULD like.'

'Is he a politician?'

'He is a Paramount Chief.'

'That sounds all right."

'Yes, it is ALL right,' Henry agreed, practically falling apart with laughter, although, to be fair, his amusement this time may have been aroused by the object on the wheel, which now looked like a cross between the Tower of Pisa and a pregnant woman.

'Odd chap, Henry,' Martin said, when he had finished explaining to me how the kiln worked and also presented me with an ashtray as a souvenir. It was rather attractive, in a muted way, and weighed about half a ton.

'Most unusual, I would have said.'

'Oh, would you? I hope he wasn't spinning a lot of yarns?' Martin asked, staring at me with a burning intensity. 'He's rather apt to romanticise and you shouldn't take him too seriously. He doesn't set out deliberately to mislead, you understand. It's simply that where he comes from it's considered good manners to tell people what you believe they wish to hear.'

'Well, he believed I wished to hear that he was the son of a Paramount Chief, whatever that may be. Isn't it true?'

Martin gave one of his impatient snorts, which sounded as though someone had pulled a cork out of his larynx.

'Could be, but highly improbable, I should say. The fact is, Henry knows no more about it than the rest of us.'

'Why's that?'

'He's an orphan. Adopted and brought up by missionaries. They cottoned on that he was a bright lad and they got him into one of the best schools in the country. He did pretty well there too. Lots of bits of paper to show he's passed this and that.'

I squinted down at the ashtray, which required both hands to hold, saying:

'This isn't meant to be rude because I feel sure it takes an awful lot of brains and skill to be a potter, but I wouldn't have thought it was a particularly intellectual pursuit. I wonder why he chose it?'

'Because he's an opportunist, old Henry, that's why,' Martin said with another of his alarming snorts. 'He was training to be a doctor, but some philanthropic enterprise was handing out fellowships in pottery, and he saw it as a chance for a free trip to Europe. They pay all his expenses and tuition for a year.'

'And do you have to accept anyone they choose to land on you?'

'Good heavens, no. They're all very thoroughly vetted. This outfit who provide the wherewithal has some tie-up with the Benson-Jones empire. Magnus takes a personal interest in all the candidates. Quite a lot of our students come to us in that way. Walter is another of them, and he's really dedicated. Funny business, really; Henry's got twice the talent and yet it would have been all the same to him if they'd been offering fellowships in fish farming, I daresay.'

'Except that in this job he can at least wear his white coat. I expect that makes him feel like a doctor.'

Martin glanced at me sharply. 'You could be right, at that. He's a fanciful chap. Enterprising too. Hadn't been here above a week when he asked for a couple of days off to go to London. I guessed he was a bit short of cash, so I asked him how he meant to get there and he said he'd walk. Did too. Set off hours before daylight on Monday morning, and strolled in on Tuesday night as fresh as a daisy. Over a hundred miles there and back, you know. I daresay he cadged a few lifts on the way but you have to hand it to him. Another thing . . .'

I never discovered what the other thing was because at that point there was a lot of bangle jangling as Babs came swooping down on us with the news that Julie and Kit were ready to leave. She walked out to the car with me and asked how long I was staying.

'Only till tomorrow evening, when my chore will be done. Besides, my husband is coming back from Paris tomorrow and I can't wait to see him.'

'I'm so glad to hear you say that,' she said in a soupy voice.

I found it an inappropriate comment too, but there was more to come.

'What I mean is, Tessa, it's a relief to find you're such a devoted pair. I'm thinking of Sarah, naturally.'

'What's she got to do with it?'

'Just that she happens to be very deeply in love with Kit and, from the way he talks about you, Martin and I were so afraid there might be something in the wind.'

'Lord no. We're not even particularly good friends. It's simply that when you work with someone every day for weeks on end they tend to crop up rather frequently in your conversation. I do it myself, but it doesn't mean a thing and Robin knows that. Once this picture is in the can, Kit and I will go our separate ways again.'

'Thank you, you've really put my mind at rest.'

'You're very concerned about Sarah?'

'Well naturally, my dear. They're the only family in these parts that one finds much in common with. Also I admire her tremendously. She has so much integrity, you know, and she wouldn't be the kind to fall in love with just anyone. We'd hate it to go wrong now that she's at last found someone she can be happy with.'

'Yes, I expect you would.'

'She's led such an unnatural life ever since her mother died. We feel it's high time she broke out of her father's orbit.'

Irritated by this blatant insincerity, I said: 'It doesn't follow that she will. Whoever Sarah marries, she'll always put her father first. We've seen an example of that this morning. However, I agree with you that it would be a pity if she broke it off with Kit because he is probably one of the very few who would tolerate the situation. In fact, it's probably his principal asset, so far as Sarah is concerned.'

I have never quite understood what made me lay it on the line quite so squarely for her. Perhaps it was her sanctimonious hypocrisy which provoked me into speaking so plainly, but whatever the reason I had good cause to remember my words later.

2

On the return journey Kit was at the wheel, with Julie squashed in between him and myself which, for reasons quite distinct from those which had dictated it, turned out to be a fortunate arrangement. She was so practised in the art of shrinking into a small, unobtrusive ball that when the emergency came Kit had at least ample room to manoeuvre, which probably contributed to the saving of life and limb although he did show commendable coolness as well.

It happened as we approached the gates of Eglinton Hall. We heard the roar of a motor cycle coming down the drive and a few seconds later the driver flashed into view, making a wide, racing sweep to the right, in order to turn left, at the precise moment when Kit was beginning his own turn in. Instead of switching course, he continued turning and turning until he had made a complete circle. The motor cycle wavered, righted itself again and shot past our stern as we landed up, petrified but unharmed, facing the way we had come.

We sat there in numbed silence, while the roar of the motor bike gradually faded to a distant crackle, Kit's head thrown back, as though silently addressing a word of thanks to the Almighty, and Julie's bowed over her lap.

'He could have killed himself,' I said at last. 'And us too. Who was it? Do you know, Julie?'

'It was Walter—I think.'

'Does he always drive like that?'

'No, that is, I don't think so . . .'

'Will you report him?'

She raised her head at this. 'Well, no. I mean, there's no need, is there? No one's hurt.'

'But he was driving like a lunatic,' I complained, nervous reaction making me irritable. 'We could all have been killed, if Kit hadn't kept his head.'

'I'm beginning to regret it now,' Kit said, switching on the ignition again. 'He's the one who would have copped it if there had been a collision, and nothing would please me more. He's a menace, that Walter.'

'Isn't that what I keep telling you?'

'But I'm sure he didn't mean any harm, Tessa,' Julie said imploringly. 'He was probably a bit upset . . . just wasn't thinking.'

'And he just wasn't thinking during that little punch up last night,' Kit remarked sourly. 'Or so he would have us believe.'

'What does that mean?'

'Only that however loudly he says he mistook me for one of the yobs, he knew damn well who I was. He must have. I was lying on my back, having practically passed out, if you want to know. I heard a rustling noise, so I dragged my eyes open, and there he was, standing quite close and looking down at me. Then he hauled me up, just for the thrill of knocking me down again. He's really disturbed, I'd say.'

'I call it worse than that. Could anyone really be so point-lessly savage?'

'I don't know,' Julie said unhappily. 'If Kit says so . . . You see, poor Walter's rather an emotional sort of person . . . a bit unbalanced in some ways. I mean, you saw him just now.'

'Yes, but presumably that wasn't deliberate. It doesn't explain why he should set on Kit.'

'Oh, didn't you know, Tessa? I'm the dreaded rival. I expect he'd have killed me, if he'd dared.'

'Rival for what?'

'The hand of Miss Sarah Benson-Jones, of course. What else?'

'You're joking!'

'You tell her, Julie.'

'Well, it's too ridiculous, you know, Tessa, but there is a grain of truth in it. Walter's got the most terrific crush on Sarah.'

'Really? He concealed it pretty well last night.'

'Maybe so, but I think it was mainly to impress her that he went tearing off in pursuit of the attacker. He was always hanging around at one time, until she got bored with it and told him to push off, and I suppose it's better for his ego to pretend that everything would have been different if it weren't for Kit.'

'She's probably had to sort him out again this morning,' Kit remarked. 'Hence the performance just now.'

'So, you see, it's best not to stir up any more trouble than we can help,' Julie pleaded. 'You never know what the press might ferret out if Walter were to be prosecuted. It's not the kind of publicity to benefit any of us, least of all Kit.'

'Whereas, by keeping quiet, someone else may get hurt during one of his tantrums. However, I suppose that doesn't bother you?'

'Tessa's a real little tiger for law and order, isn't she Julie? That's what comes of marrying into the fuzz, so be warned. Don't go falling for any blue eyed policemen.' Julie giggled delightedly, which infuriated me still further, and I said sharply:

'No danger of that. The way things are going, she won't be lucky enough to meet any. I suppose one of you may call them in when Walter actually kills someone, but I wouldn't care to bet on it.'

'Oh goodness me, how you exaggerate, Tessa,' Julie said with more giggles. 'I'm sure it's not as desperate as that. Walter will get over it soon and find someone suitable to fall in love with. It's just that he's rather impetuous and he's going through a difficult time.'

I was growing crosser by the minute and Kit's snide remark about Robin still rankled. We had arrived at the house by then but before getting out of the car I said, with as much contempt as I could fling into it:

'I expect you're right. We all know what fools unrequited love can make of people.'

3

On the lawn outside the window which had been the centre of the previous night's fraças a red and white striped tent had been erected, and Sarah was standing beside it, talking to two men in dungarees. She left them when she saw the car and walked over to us, all the cares of the world on her shoulders by the look of it.

'It seems we'll have to wait ages to get the window mended. Isn't it sickening? They're not standard panes and they'll have to be cut specially. Apparently, there isn't a soul in the village who can do it, and we haven't a hope of getting an outside firm during the holiday. George and Alf suggested boarding it up in the meantime, but won't that make the room look so ghastly from inside? What do you honestly think, Tessa?'

As usual, she seemed to hang on my answer, and endeavouring to oblige I said:

'I'd leave it as it is. I imagine we'll be mostly out of doors anyway.'

'Yes, that's true, and it would look much more noticeable boarded up, don't you agree, Julie? Would you be an angel and ask them to remove the broken glass and leave the rest as it is? Come along, Tessa, I want to show you Madame Rosetta's headquarters. Don't you think it's rather fetching?' she asked, taking my arm and leading me towards the tent.

'What mystifies me,' I remarked, 'is how you find as many willing hands as you do on Good Friday. The director of our picture would love to know your secret.'

'Oh, but these are not our own people,' she told me in shocked tones. 'Good heavens no; we shouldn't dream of asking them to work over the holiday. They're all from local building firms and so on. Quite pleased to weigh in on an occasion like this and earn a little extra.'

The ethics of this arrangement eluded me, unless of course it implied that the Eglinton Hall staff were all out earning overtime with the local building firms, and I switched my attention to an inspection of Madame Rosetta's tent.

There was a large signboard propped up outside it, depicting an open palm criss-crossed with thick black lines, and it had two flaps to provide an entrance and an exit, both of which were now pulled back. Inside there was a table covered by a dark green woollen cloth which hung down to the floor and on it was a crystal ball beside some unopened packs of cards.

There was really nothing to be said, either for or against it but Sarah, as usual, was frowning at me and begging for constructive comments, so in desperation I said: 'Perhaps the cards are too new? They might look more authentic if they were a bit thumbed and greasy.'

'How right you are,' she replied, 'and how lucky you noticed it! Now, where on earth . . . ?'

The problem of finding a used pack of cards had obviously cast her into fresh turmoils of indecision and to calm her down I asked her how much she proposed to charge her customers.

'Twenty five? Or do you think that's too much?'

'I'll be able to tell you when you've read my palm.'

'Half price for children, you know. Now, I wonder if the Grahams would have some old packs of cards they could lend me? I think I'll get Julie to ring up and ask.'

'If not, I expect Walter would be prepared to fly round the countryside and hold people up to ransom for them.'

'Why Walter?'

'We almost ran into him. He was skimming down your drive at a hundred miles an hour.'

'How extraordinary! Are you sure it was Walter?'

'So Julie said.'

'Well, she must have been mistaken. Walter hasn't been near the place. I've been here myself ever since I left you, except for a couple of minutes on the telephone. Oh, damn! Oh, Tessa, do forgive me! I completely forgot to tell you.'

'What?'

'The telephone call; it went right out of my head. Goodness, how dreadful of me! I'm most terribly sorry.' She looked so utterly distraught that only one explanation occurred to me.

'Was it Robin? Has something happened to him?'

'Oh no, nothing like that. It was your cousin. He said his name was Toby Crichton.'

'Oh yes, Toby.'

'He said it wasn't urgent but that you'd know the number if you felt like calling him back.'

'Yes, I will, if you don't mind. He lives not far away; well, only about ten miles, and I've told him he must come over tomorrow and swell the takings.'

'Oh, super! That's simply marvellous, Tessa. And listen, why not ask him to come for lunch? We all adore his plays and Magnus would be thrilled to meet him. Come along inside and ring him up right away.'

She was certainly an impeccable hostess, neglecting no opportunity to flatter and cosset the guest, and yet it was hard to believe that such a dramatic build up for a most unsensational telephone call had been entirely guileless. Whatever else, it had very effectively swept the subject of Walter under the carpet.

CHAPTER SIX

1

MAGNUS also denied all knowledge of Walter's visit, when the subject was reopened several hours later. He had spent the whole day in his own apartments, presumably sorting out the muddles of Munich, and did not burst upon us until just before dinner. The bandage by then had been replaced by a wad of lint held in place with sticking plaster.

'Just a very simple dinner,' Sarah had explained to me apologetically. 'I do hope you won't mind, but they're all up to their eyes in the kitchen with buns and cakes for tomorrow.'

Curiously enough, she was wearing the identical acid green trouser suit, which had looked so harsh and unbecoming on Julie the night before. Julie, on the other hand, had elected to put on the identical maroon one, in which she succeeded in looking merely drab, so I was more thankful than ever to have opted out of this particular contest.

In fact, I had rather skimped on the grande toilette that evening, having spent the hour before dinner pottering to and fro between my bedroom and bathroom while I ran through the speech in my head. I had been faintly annoyed to discover that, despite Magnus's assurance, the pompous peroration had been retained intact and unaltered in the final version, proving either that his flair for detail was not quite so highly developed as he imagined or else that in retyping it Sarah had ignored his instructions. Whatever the reason, I did not intend to let them get away with it but meanwhile, being quite accustomed to delivering other people's lines, however silly, I automatically committed that passage to memory, along with the rest, meaning to attack Magnus about it as soon as the opportunity arose.

In the event I never did so, for other more pressing matters were soon to obtrude and push it out of my mind.

Had it not been for the conspiracy of silence which had wrapped itself like a cocoon round the mysterious motor cyclist, the incident might have faded into the background, but in fact I only waited for Magnus to ask me if I was enjoying myself to bring him up to date on this matter.

'Apart from that rather unpleasant experience, everything's been lovely,' I concluded.

He had been looking from me to Julie in apparent bewilderment during my recital, and once again I had the impression that Sarah, without once glancing in our direction, was listening to every word.

'How very distressing!' Magnus said. 'Are you sure it was Walter, Julie?'

'No, I'm not. Poor Walter, I'm afraid I did him an injustice. I assumed it was him because he's the only person we know who rides one of those machines; but people all look alike in their helmets and goggles, don't they? I expect it was someone who turned down here by mistake, thinking it was a lane, and then got in a panic when he realised he was on private property.'

She paused, and a strange silence fell over the whole party. In the course of it a brief look passed between Sarah and Julie, and Julie said:

'In fact, I'm positive now that it can't have been Walter because when I telephoned Babs about borrowing some playing cards she mentioned that he'd gone over to spend the day with a friend in Oxford. He left immediately after breakfast.'

2

'And if it hadn't been for the last bit I might have fallen for it,' I admitted. 'Inexperienced liars always mess things up by over-elaborating.'

'How do you know she's inexperienced?' Toby asked.

He had arrived at Eglinton Hall just after midday on Saturday which, strictly speaking, was a little early for a luncheon engagement but it had come about through a combination of circumstances for which I was largely responsible. Sarah had impressed upon me that lunch would be served punctually, to enable us to be in our places on the platform by half past two, and knowing his dilatory ways I had lopped half an hour off this time, as well as greatly exaggerating the distance from Roakes Common. Evidently, I was such an experienced liar that I had slightly under-elaborated, and he had walked into the house about an hour before anyone expected him.

Since by this time Magnus was escorting the judges round the fruit and vegetable exhibits, Kit and Sarah were in the meadow setting up posts for the musical pony ride and Julie was supervising the layout of the tombola prizes, it fell to me to entertain him, and I had begun with a tour of the house and garden, no doubt displaying all the ridiculous pride of ownership of the guest of twenty four hours' standing in the presence of an even newer arrival. At any rate he had rapidly become bored to smithereens by this performance, as well as worn out by the physical slog, so I had led him to a seat in the shade of a cedar tree and had attempted to divert him with tales of life chez Benson-Jones. This was much more up his street, for he was always passionately interested in people he scarcely knew and was unlikely to meet again, and he listened with gratifying absorption to my descriptions of the flying brick, the intricate family relationships and the mad motor cyclist, to name but three of the subjects I brought out for his inspection.

'How do you know she's inexperienced?' he asked again, since I had hesitated over answering the question on the first time round.

'It's hard to explain, Toby, but you may see what I mean when you meet her. It's not that she's retarded exactly, but I think she's been over protected because of her illness. She's so naive, too. Take this crush she's got on Kit. You wouldn't expect a child of ten to be so blatant about it, and yet I don't believe she has the slightest idea that anyone has caught on.'

'Do you suppose it bothers Sarah at all?'

'Oh, I shouldn't think she takes it seriously. That's half the trouble. They're only a few minutes apart in age, but she behaves to Julie like a bossy headmistress who's made a pet of one of the pupils.'

'Which may be why the pupil has never grown up?'

'Exactly; although Sarah herself is rather immature in some ways. All this clamouring for approval and reassurance must mean a basic insecurity of some kind, and yet it's hard to see the reason for it. The only thing she seems positive about is that she'll marry Kit and still keep on running her father's affairs, with Julie as the errand boy.'

'It sounds very daft, but one has to remember that no one who was completely sane would dream of marrying the Kitbag.'

'I agree, and he's another case. Honestly, Toby, I don't know what to say about Kit.'

'Well, that makes a change.'

'He's turning out to be such a dual personality. At the studios he's the complete extrovert, ever so matey and democratic with all the technicians and showing off like mad, but with this lot he's completely subdued. And he got absolutely stoned the other night. It was quite a shock because normally he can take any amount without turning a hair.'

'Perhaps the idea of marrying Sarah has gone sour on him and he hasn't the nerve to tell her so?'

'I shouldn't wonder. He was probably dazzled by all the power and riches and, not being very sophisticated, imagined that he was carrying off the prize of the century. Whereas any man in his senses would have swum the Atlantic sooner than get caught in her net.'

'Isn't swimming the Atlantic more or less what he intends?'

I was unable to bring him up to date on this topic because Magnus came bounding up to introduce the secretary of the local branch of the conservationists. He was an aquiline dyspeptic looking man named Dr Simmons, who turned out to be the very one whom Sarah had been so anxious to placate, and I could tell that in this instance there were grounds for trepidation. However, his disagreeable manner may have been merely the protective colouring of one who had learnt to be on his guard against the perfect stranger's request for free medical advice and so, leaving Toby, the world's foremost hypochondriac, to show him just how tough life could be, I walked ahead with Magnus. He was sportily attired for the occasion in white trousers and dark blue blazer and was demonstrating the benefits of his gymnastic apparatus by striding forth like an Olympic champion. One of the adhesive strips on his surgical dressing had stopped adhering and he kept pressing it back into place, which reminded me to ask him:

'By the way, how did you come by that cut? It might be as well to know.'

He laughed and patted my arm. 'Oh, didn't I tell you? Some Bank Holiday revellers came up to the house the other night after the pubs had closed and bunged a stone through the window. I happened to be standing in the line of fire.'

'Hard cheese!'

'Wasn't it? Luckily, it was only a graze; and it may provide you with a valuable tip.'

'I can't imagine how.'

'When putting out a story for public consumption, always stick as near to the truth as possible.'

'Thank you,' I replied, 'but I knew that already. My husband would add that it puts us in the top bracket of the criminal classes.'

CHAPTER SEVEN

1

AT HALF past two, when the band of the local Fire Brigade launched into the opening bars of 'Bonnie and Clyde', the grass verge bordering the drive was already thick with cars, and by the time the official party mounted the platform a crowd of several hundred was gathered below it. I was installed in the front row between Magnus and Dr Simmons, while Sarah and Julie sat behind with Kit, Sarah now attired as a startlingly clean and affluent gypsy, complete with plunging neckline, immense gold earrings and scarlet buckled shoes.

As I stood up to begin my speech, a trifling, but none-theless annoying hitch occurred. I had already noticed that the group of cameramen who made up the front row of the audience had been joined at the last minute by Henry. In fact, his arrival had caused quite a stir, because he had jostled his way through from the back and had then plopped down cross-legged on the grass, placed an enormous tartan hold-all at his feet and smiled benignly up at us, as though signalling for the proceedings to begin.

I realised afterwards that Sarah must have been strung up to the highest pitch of nervous agitation and that this triv-ial incident had snapped the last thread of her self-control, for with no warning at all she went into action. There was a rustle of gypsy petticoats as she left her seat and went down the wooden steps to the lawn, pushing her outstretched arms before her in shoo-ing movements, like one turning back a flock of geese. Punctuated by murmurs and giggles from the audience, she stood with her back to us talking to Henry who gazed up at her with mournful, questioning eyes. For a minute or so it looked like stalemate, but finally he got to his feet and began to push his way back through the crowd. His progress was accompanied by laughter and a few sporadic outbursts of applause from the crowd, but it did not appear to be malicious, and indeed several of those nearest to him smiled and patted his shoulder as he passed. Nevertheless it had been an embarrassing episode and no one looked more conscious of the fact than Sarah herself as she returned to the platform. Magnus did not so much as glance at her but continued with a frowning scrutiny of his finger nails, although it was probably I who most deplored Henry's departure. It is such a useful trick to single out one member of an audience who appears to be paying attention and to address oneself exclusively to him, and Henry had shown every indication of being ideally suited for this role.

Fortunately I soon found a substitute in Martin Graham. He was standing in the fourth or fifth row, but even so I could see his glinting, fanatical eye fastened upon me. Responding with a matching concentration, I blazed through the whole speech without a single fluff and did not realise until I was well into it that the silly, platitudinous final passage was also getting an airing.

Despite all this drivel, I got quite a good hand, although Magnus managed to upstage me and get an even bigger one by showering me with kisses and bravos, bringing loud applause from the voters. These antics concluded, a portly female of about three years old was shovelled up on to the platform by an over-anxious adult and eventually prevailed upon to hand over a bunch of carnations before being led away, yelling at the top of her lungs about the injustice of it all.

Magnus then made a brief announcement, urging all present to enjoy themselves and spend a lot of money, and I was hauled off by scowling Simmons to be introduced to the winners of the produce competitions.

This concluded my official duties and, predictably enough, everyone instantly lost interest in me and became immersed in their own busy lives. Even Toby had deserted me although I did finally run him to earth near Madame Rosetta's tent. In the meantime, I had acquired scores of raffle tickets, guessed the name of the doll, the weight of the cake and the number of beans in the jar, had staked out my claim for the buried treasure and also patronised Julie's tombola. There I drew four blanks and the number thirteen, which lived up to its reputation by providing me with a bottle of ginger wine. Moreover, as she had a bevy of capable women assisting her, plus assorted cubs and brownies, the whole transaction only used up half a minute, and time had now become the most expendable commodity.

'You wouldn't have any change?' Julie asked me. 'We're running short.'

'It's worse than that,' I admitted. 'I've no money left at all. I was going to ask if I could pay for my strawberry tea by cheque.'

'I must go indoors and get some,' she said, taking a handful of notes from her cash box. 'I'm leaving you in charge, Mrs Parry, but I'll be as quick as I can.'

'Luckily, Sarah thinks of everything,' she explained to me, as we walked away. 'She's stashed twenty pounds' worth of silver in the downstairs cloakroom.'

'I'll fetch it for you, if you like,' I said. 'I'd welcome a job. I feel rather superfluous at the moment.'

'You shouldn't. You've done your bit and can afford to rest on your laurels.'

'It's about the only thing left which I can afford.'

We had reached the house by this time but instead of going inside she turned her back on the door, and I had the distinct impression of being seen off. It was reinforced when she said, with one of her sideways glances:

'If you're serious about wanting a job, Tessa, perhaps you could go and cast an eye on Henry?'

'Why? What's he up to?'

'Apparently, he's already won the pig in the bowling competition and there are rumours that he's favourite for the cockerel in the dart throwing.'

'It sounds as though he's doing quite well without any help from me.'

'That's the trouble. The local champions may not feel too happy about being trounced by an . . .'

'African?'

'Outsider, I was going to say, a term which includes someone from the next village, incidentally. Perhaps you could draw him off, in a tactful way? You could point out that Babs might not be too pleased to have all this livestock on the premises. I'll leave it to you, though, because I must see about this change. Mrs Parry will be having kittens if I leave her much longer.'

Abandoned once more, I ambled across to the darts enclosure, where a cloud no bigger than Australia was hanging over the proceedings. A few gloomy looking spectators were leaning on the ropes, but neither Henry nor anyone else was playing. The scorer's expression as I approached indicated a revival of hope that there was one born every minute.

'Want to try your luck? Three for a bob, and ladies stand half way up the pitch. Come on, now! Have a go!' I found a fivepenny piece in my parking meter purse and accepted the three darts. The first one struck the wooden mount, the second actually found the board and the third sailed over the top of it and fell to earth I know not where. I had scored a total of eight.

'Hardly worth writing it down?' I suggested.

"You could have another try. Only a hundred and forty to beat.'

'No thanks, I'm not quite in that class.'

'That's what they all say. Not very good for business, is it? Might as well shut up shop, with only a couple of quid in the kitty. That's a laugh for you! We took going on eighty last year.'

'What you need are some consolation prizes for the runners-up. I expect it can be arranged. Hang on a bit and I'll try and organise something.'

Julie had not returned to her post, so I was unable to consult her, but in any case it presented itself as just the kind of problem that Sarah would enjoy worrying over, and I therefore set off in quest of a prophecy or two from Madame Rosetta. It was then that I met Toby, walking thoughtfully away from her tent.

'Any good?' I asked him.

'Quite remarkable,' he admitted. 'She's the real thing. Do you know, she told me I was destined to meet a dark stranger who would alter the course of my life, and by the most astonishing coincidence I did. A very dark stranger indeed, and he seemed to know his role too, for he immediately got into conversation on the pretext of asking the time. I can't honestly say that it has made much difference to my life so far, but it's early days.'

'Give him time,' I said. 'He's capable of anything. And this particular dark stranger is the very one I seek.'

Toby waved his hand in the direction of the tent and, remembering just in time to borrow some money from him, I proceeded on my way.

Babs was waiting outside and I asked her if she would mind my jumping the queue.

'I need only two minutes,' I promised her, 'but there's a bit of future that needs immediate sorting out if we're to stave off financial disaster and international incidents.'

'Quite all right with me, my dear, I've had my go.'

'Oh really? Did she tell you anything nice?'

'No, she didn't tell me anything at all. I only went in to make the gesture. I think it's a load of rubbish and I'm afraid I told her so.'

'Did she mind?'

'Not a bit. She was dying to go to the bathroom, and she asked me to stop here and keep everyone at bay for five minutes, while she nipped indoors through the drawing room window.'

'And then what?'

Babs opened her baby blue eyes. 'Then nothing. No one came near the place for at least ten minutes, so it would have made no difference if I'd waited or not.'

'I mean, why are you still hanging around?'

'Oh, because just as I was leaving Henry turned up, and he's in a funny mood. I was afraid Sarah might have a bit of trouble with him.'

'What sort of funny?'

'Excited. He's pathetically gullible about all this kind of thing, you know. He's got it firmly fixed in his head that Sarah really does possess supernatural powers. I can't get it through to him that it's meant to be a kind of joke.'

'Well, I'd back Sarah to handle him,' I said, with a confidence which got badly dented a moment later when Henry came blundering out of the tent, giving every sign of being still in the grip of the funny mood. He stared at us both without apparent recognition.

'Are you all right, Henry?' Babs asked doubtfully.

'She is NOT there,' he replied in a rather dazed voice. 'No one is there.'

'You don't mean she hasn't come back? What on earth can she be doing?' Babs asked, impatiently pulling aside the entrance flap and sticking her head inside.

'Are you there, Sarah?' she called. 'Is anything wrong?'

The moment her back was turned Henry smiled at me in a puzzled way, and then abruptly streaked off in the direction of the cedar tree.

'It's quite true, my dear,' Babs told me, evidently too annoyed to notice that he had gone. 'She simply hasn't bothered to come back. Isn't that typical? She does exactly what she thinks she will.'

'Unlike me,' I said, walking past her into the tent for a personal inspection. 'I so often find myself doing exactly what I think I won't.'

'You can see for yourself,' Babs said, joining me in the tent. 'God knows what she expects me to do about it.'

'Well, cheer up, because I don't think she's gone very far.'

I was peering ahead of me, but as I said this I heard a sharp clash of bracelets and when I turned round I saw that Babs was rummaging around in her bag.

'What do you mean "not very far"?' she asked in a distant voice, bringing out her cigarettes and lighter. 'How can you tell?'

'She's left her shoes behind, or one of them at any rate. It's over by the back entrance. One of those red buckled affairs.'

'Oh well, that accounts for it, I suppose,' Babs said, sounding merely bored now and walking out of the tent. 'Probably they were too tight and she's gone to fetch some others. Where's Henry?'

'He left about five minutes ago.'

'Oh damn I I'd better see if I can find him. He's supposed to be helping Martin on the display stand. Will you stay here and hold the fort? It looks as though we have some customers coming.'

There were three of them, advancing across the grass towards us, a man with two women, who both wore flowered hats and were both talking at the same time as they gazed adoringly up at their companion. He was loving every minute of it too, laughing and throwing his head back, in the well known gesture which so frequently had a thousand teenagers swooning in the aisles.

Their merriment cooled somewhat as they became aware of spectators and the women became rather self-conscious under our scrutiny. Evidently, Babs knew them, for she went up and spoke to them and after a bit of argument all three walked away.

'Pathetic old pussies,' Kit remarked. 'What's going on here?'

'Nothing. Sarah seems to be taking her tea break. I've been instructed to wait until she returns. Have you handed out your silver cups and rosettes yet?'

'No, that's not until five thirty. I can spare you a moment of my precious company. What a foul way to spend an afternoon, wouldn't you say?'

'It could be raining, I suppose.'

'With Sarah and her Dad in charge? You have to be joking! Shall we go inside? It's getting bloody cold out here.'

'It's not all that cosy in the tent, but I suppose we could sit down. I'll consult the crystal ball and see if there are any Oscars floating around in your aura.'

As it happened they were the last light hearted words I was to utter for several hours for no supernatural powers were needed to show that, whatever the future might hold for the rest of us, there was none left for Sarah. As I approached her chair behind the table I saw the pair to the discarded shoe, and her foot was still in it.

She lay on her back, her head and shoulders at an unnaturally curved angle, as though she had arched herself in a last tremendous convulsion as death overtook her. The grass around her was stained with blood and the feathers and shaft of a dart were sticking out above the neckline of her dress.

2

There followed an interval of utter madness, in which the Benson-Jones publicity phobia entered a new dimension although the nightmare started before that, with my long and frustrated attempts to find one of them and break the news.

Leaving Kit in charge, I had taken on this task myself, seeing it as the lesser evil, but after only ten minutes would gladly have settled for sitting it out to eternity with half a dozen corpses, sooner than jostle my hopeless way through apathetic crowds to the accompaniment of a selection from 'The Sound of Music', interminably asking whether anyone had seen Sir Magnus or Julie. Mostly the response was an indifferent negative, and eventually I came to prefer this to the counter enquiries I received from people who tried to be helpful. It was not really possible to explain to them that a close relative had been stabbed to death in one of the amusement tents, and I was too numbed with shock to invent a plausible alternative.

Even Mrs Parry was useless, for she told me in martyred tones that Julie had not returned and that she could not sell me any more tickets unless I gave her the right money. I unloaded all the silver I had plundered from Toby and struck off towards the house.

Curiously enough it was Walter who finally put an end to this grotesque situation. I met him coming out of the downstairs cloakroom and although he was not the port I would have chosen in this particular storm the sight of a familiar face, even such a red and truculent one, was a haven of a kind.

'Is Julie in there?' I asked him.

'Julie? Why no, she's not,' he replied, looking understandably taken aback.

'You wouldn't have any idea where I could find her, I suppose?'

'Sorry, Ma'am, I only just arrived. Been spending the night over in Oxford, and it was quite a party. Consequence was I . . .'

'And Sir Magnus? You don't know where he is either?'

'Why yes, I'd say he was upstairs in his room.'

'Do you know that for a fact? This is really urgent.'

'I couldn't absolutely swear to it,' he replied ponderously, 'but what happened was like this, see. I came in here because I was planning on making a telephone call, but it turned out there was someone on the line. Naturally, I put the phone down, soon as I realised, but it was Sir Magnus's voice all right. The way I see it, he would have to be in his room if he . . .'

'Thanks,' I called, already half way up the stairs by this time, and continuing at such a rate that it was only when I reached Magnus's door and raised my hand to knock that the full horror of the ordeal ahead at last caught up with me. Taking an enormous breath, I rapped on the door and burst into the room.

It was quite true that he was speaking on the telephone but he heard me coming and swivelled round, covering the mouthpiece with his hand. For an instant he looked so fierce that I felt a wave of relief, believing he must already have heard the news and was telephoning the authorities. It was not so, however, for his expression cleared at once and he said genially:

'Ah, it's you! Do come in. This is a tiresome business call, but I'll be with you in a minute. I want to hear how everything's going.'

'I'm sorry, Magnus, but I have some terrible news for you, and it can't wait. There's been an accident. It's very bad, and you've got to prepare yourself. I'd have brought Julie, but I couldn't find her, so you'll have to hear it from me.'

I suppose my mention of Julie brought it home to him that the accident was to Sarah, for his hand shook as he replaced the receiver and then waited for me to continue.

It took only a minute and he heard me out in silence, while the muscles of his face sagged and all the vibrancy went out of him. When I had finished he fought hard to control himself, pressing his finger tips against his temples and then slowly pushing them upwards into his hair. Recalling the scene now, my principal memory is of the scar standing out like a scarlet thread against the greyish pallor of the surrounding skin.

'I'll come at once,' he said, flattening the palm of his hand on the desk to lever himself up.

'You don't think . . . ?'

'What?'

Twice already that weekend I had found myself urging people to notify the police, and I quailed at the prospect of another repetition.

'That you should put out a call for Dr Simmons?' I said, finding a compromise.

'But you say she's dead?'

'Yes.'

'Then first I must see her. The rest can be done later.'

I could tell that he was quite determined and I said reluctantly:

'Then we had better go out through the drawing room window. It's quicker.'

'And we're less likely to be seen,' he agreed, chilling my blood by adding softly: 'And we have to think of that.'

*

Julie had joined Kit in the tent when we reached it. They were seated side by side on the grass, with the table between them and Sarah's body. Ignoring them both, Magnus knelt down beside Sarah, taking her hand in his and gently smoothing back the tousled hair from her forehead. We waited in respectful silence until he stood up, staring in a puzzled way at the blood on his hands and saying:

'We must try and move her into the house as unobtrusively as possible. Kit and I will carry her and you girls had better station yourselves, one at each entrance, and pass the word when it's all clear. Are you ready, Kit?'

'But you mustn't,' I implored him. 'I beg you not to.'

'Mustn't what?' he asked vaguely.

'Move her. I hate to say this because I know how it must pain you, but it has to be said. She has been murdered and nothing should be touched until the police get here. Apart from anything else, it would make you an accessory.'

'Ah!' he replied thoughtfully and without apparent sarcasm. 'Thank you for reminding me. I am sure you mean well, but possibly you have overlooked certain . . . considerations. I don't place myself above the law, you understand, but Sarah is my child and I'm damned if I'll leave her out here. If the police want to raise hell about it, they must do so; but I'm not without influence and I doubt if there'll be any complaint. You agree, Julie?'

She and Kit had both stood up when Magnus entered and even through deeper preoccupations I had noticed how she had mysteriously acquired a new straightness and dignity.

'I do agree,' she said, 'that we should not publicise what has happened, or ask people to leave. We don't want to start a panic, and, even more important, we don't want them blocking up the drive and preventing the ambulance and police cars from getting through.'

'Yes, a good point. And so now, if you're quite ready, Kit?'

'Wait a minute, Magnus,' Julie said, still with the same strange new authority. 'I hadn't finished. Tessa's right. I'm sure I hate to leave Sarah here quite as much as you do, but from now on our feelings aren't going to count, and we must learn to accept the fact. Even you can't break the law in a thing like this and get away with it.'

'My dear girl, I think you may safely leave that decision to me. And I shall take full responsibility, so you need have no fears on that score. Now, if you would be good enough to take a look outside, Tessa? And perhaps it would be better if you were not to come in again. You can then safely deny all knowledge of our intentions. You too, Julie, if you feel so strongly about it.'

'But there's something you've both overlooked,' I said making a last effort. 'It's not simply a question of what you can or can't get away with. Surely it's equally important to find out who did this? Personally, I don't think it's going to be at all easy, but by moving her you may destroy what evidence there is. I can't believe you would want that.'

Kit, who had not so far uttered a word, now looked at Magnus with a haggard expression and said almost in a whisper:

'I'm afraid that's true, sir.'

Magnus sighed: 'Very well, since you are all against me, I shall withdraw. You may do as you think best.'

'Thank you, my dear,' Julie said, in the gentle, faintly smug tones of a mother who has tactfully talked her little boy into handing over the carving knife. 'I shall go indoors now and telephone the police. Then I'll ask Dr Simmons to make some kind of announcement over the loud speaker. He had better ask everyone who came on foot to leave by way of the meadow, and those with cars to wait until the ambulance has passed by the spot where they're parked. He'll know how to get them to co-operate.'

Having said this, she tilted her head, possibly to spare herself another sight of Sarah, and walked out of the tent. It was quite an impressive performance, the calm, unhurried gait almost obliterating her limp, and this small but decisive victory seeming to have increased her stature by a good two inches.

CHAPTER EIGHT

1

'IMAGINE arresting Henry, of all stupid things!' I said with scorn which repetition had not blunted.

'Not arrested; he's helping the police with their enquiries,' Robin said, also for about the fifth time. Everyone remotely connected with Sarah's death had been asked to remain in the vicinity and he had joined me at Toby's house late on Saturday evening.

'We all know that it amounts to the same thing,' I retorted.

'No, we all don't. Besides, what else could they do? His prints were all over the dart and, according to the medical evidence, she must have been killed within minutes of his being in the tent. Furthermore, even you admitted that he looked a bit stunned when he came out. Mrs Graham had been so concerned about his mood that she deliberately hung around in case Sarah needed help in coping with him.'

'So she says!'

'But even if he's innocent, the chances are that Henry knows something or saw something which he hasn't yet revealed.'

'Added to which he's a stranger, and a coloured one at that, which makes it easier to cut a few corners.'

'You're not seriously suggesting that they wouldn't have acted in precisely the same way if he'd been a local boy?'

'No, not really, Robin, but you can't get away from the fact that it would cause a lot less dismay round the parish pump if Henry were arrested, rather than say Walter.'

'No doubt; and on the same principle I daresay there are a few in Harlem or Notting Hill Gate who would have equally irrational reasons for wishing to see Walter in the same spot. The point is that, so far as anyone knows, Walter wasn't anywhere near when the murder was committed. Whereas Henry not only was, but is displaying all the signs of a guilty conscience.'

'Or fear. Because he's no fool and he can probably see as well as I can that whoever is behind this deliberately set out to frame him. In the first place, I don't believe it was the dart which killed her. That's mainly why I made such a fuss about their moving her.'

Robin looked interested: 'Why don't you think it was the dart?'

'I doubt if the spike would have been long enough. I may not be a forensic expert, but I have learnt a few things about human anatomy over the years.'

'It can't be entirely ruled out, although I agree that it would probably have taken a fair degree of medical knowledge to have picked exactly the right spot, if it was the dart.'

'But that's not my only objection, Robin. The real point is that there wouldn't have been any blood. How could there have been?'

'How indeed? I've been asking myself the same question. We'll have to wait for the autopsy to confirm it, but I wouldn't mind betting that some quite different weapon was used.

So why bring in the dart at all. You'll no doubt tell me that it was planted there, with Henry's prints all over it, purely to incriminate him, but isn't that over simplifying it? The murderer must have realised that the experts wouldn't be fooled for a moment.'

'Nevertheless, Henry has been arrested.'

'Held for questioning. And I think I know why, Tessa. There could be quite a different explanation for the presence of the dart, a lot more damaging and a lot more plausible. This will probably send you soaring through the roof, but the fact is that he is an African, with a totally different background from the rest of us.'

'I am aware of it,' I said coldly.

'And there's just a chance that he planted the dart there as a kind of signature. It was obvious that he'd worked himself up into a state of excitement over this witchcraft caper and, so far from wishing to conceal the deed, he might actually have wanted to advertise it.'

'Hardly, since he has subsequently denied having anything to do with it. At least, I assume he has. Otherwise the police wouldn't be fooling around with euphemisms. They'd have charged him.'

'I meant that he might have been in that state of mind at the time. One wouldn't necessarily expect the mood to last. In the cold, clear dawn of the police station, he could well have had second thoughts.'

'But all this is just surmise on your part, and based, if I may say so, purely on prejudice.'

'You may say what you like, my darling, but the fact is that I've had far more direct contact with people of Henry's background than you have, and in some respects they are different from us. Personally, I'm all in favour of it.'

'That's still no reason why they should be treated differently. I happen to like old Henry and I don't believe for one moment that he's a murderer. You'll say that's just a personal opinion, but I've got much better reasons than that for believing him innocent.'

'Such as?'

'Even if he did kid himself that Sarah was a real witch, and even if she did foretell something which scared or upset him, it's still very thin. I can think of several people who had good straightforward motives for murdering her which were far stronger than that.'

2

Later that night the police dropped their euphemisms and Henry was formally arrested. This was not because the dart bore his fingerprints, for it belonged to a set of twelve which had been used in the competition, and several people had confirmed that Henry had handled nearly all of them before selecting the three of his choice. Also in his favour was the admission of the man in charge that one dart had disappeared very early in the proceedings, and there was no saying exactly when or by whom it had been removed. In addition, Babs and I were both in a position to assert that it would have been perfectly feasible for Henry to have remained inside the tent for several minutes without seeing Sarah, if she had already been dead; and the final point, which should have clinched it, was that the post mortem revealed that she had not been killed by the dart. The blade which had penetrated her heart and caused the bleeding had been in the nature of a small dagger or carving knife, which no amount of searching had so far brought to light.

Unfortunately none of this amounted to a row of beans when set against the one positive item which the police had come up with. There was nothing particularly inspired about their discovery, for they had been led straight to it by Martin's disclosure that, contrary to instructions, some unknown hand had switched on the electric kiln during the early hours of Saturday afternoon.

When the oven had cooled down sufficiently for the contents to be examined it was found that, as well as a batch of fired pottery, including my own dismal effort of Friday morning, there were some fragments which should not have been present at all. There were three of these, each estimated to have been roughly the size of a five-penny piece when new, although the intense heat had shrivelled them to half of that and had also turned them a brownish colour as though they had been rusting in the damp for many weeks. In short, they had started life as metal buttons, exactly corresponding to those on the overalls worn by the Missendale students. Not unexpectedly, in view of the fact that Henry could only produce two of the three overalls which had been issued to him, the absence of bloodstains on his clothing was now accounted for to everyone's satisfaction except my own.

CHAPTER NINE

ON MONDAY morning we returned to London, and had scarcely entered the house when Peter telephoned.

'How's Kit?' he asked, somersaulting straight into the arena.

'Bearing up, I think. Why ask me?'

'Oh, use your loaf, Tessa! Who else would I ask? Seeing it was splashed on every front page that you were also staying there, you may conceivably have noticed something about his reactions. What kind of state is he in?'

'More or less as you'd expect. Pretty furious about the whole thing.'

There was a pause, and then Peter said: 'On the level, or are you just being flippant? What I want to know is whether he'll be fit for work tomorrow, or do I have to re-do the whole schedule?'

'Would that involve a lot of expense?'

'You're so right it would. We've gone over budget already, as you well know, but the point is, it might save time and money in the end to give him a chance to get straightened out. And there's another thing. All that matiness with the unit wasn't for nothing, you know. He's pretty well dug in there, and union trouble is all I need at this stage. It's quite a worry.'

'Well, as I see it, he was in a state of shock to begin with but he seemed to pull himself out of it fairly quickly. If it's any comfort to you, I don't believe that affair was destined to run its course. I don't mean that he wasn't shattered by her death but, the way things were going I doubt if they'd have got to the altar.'

'Well that's a crumb, I suppose. Of course the act may have changed by this time tomorrow, but thanks anyway.'

After putting the telephone down some uncomfortable feelings of remorse began to creep in, and I was tempted to ring Peter back and urge him not to place too much reliance on my verdict. I refrained, however, because he had a lot on his mind and, like Henry, I had only told him what he wished to hear, which I decided would cancel out any uncharitableness towards Kit. And by Tuesday afternoon

I was vindicated for every word, Kit by then having turned in one of the best performances of his whole career.

Naturally the circumstances had called for a radical change of attitude and he had gone the whole hog and become pathetically subdued and submissive, moving about among us with a hollow-eyed dignity which was quite awe-inspiring. During the breaks he no longer larked about with his former buddies, confining himself to sad smiles and fervent handclasps whenever one of them approached with a word of sympathy and, even more satisfactory from Peter's point of view, he had no heart for improvising or throwing in bits of business of his own invention but went straight through each take exactly as rehearsed.

As a result, we were through by five o'clock, and he invited me to have a drink. There was something I wanted to ask him so I accepted at once, turning left towards the staircase when we had passed through the soundproof door which sealed off the stage. However, the quiet tragedy act was not yet over and he reproachfully touched my arm and strode off in the opposite direction, making for his dressing room where he produced a bottle of whisky and two glasses.

'Here's to us!' he said, raising his own and leaning back against the wash basin. 'Only four more days and we'll be out of here.'

'All right for some,' I told him. 'You'll be off to the States with rings on your fingers and bells on your toes. We don't all have it so good.'

'Cheer up,' he said patronisingly, 'I expect something will come your way soon. Anyway, what gives you the idea I'm going to America?'

Feeling that it would be indelicate to point out that there was no longer anything to prevent him, I said:

'Oh, just something you told me yourself about five million times.'

'I've reconsidered,' he said, pouring more whisky into his glass and filling it from the tap. 'I have this idea I might spend a few months in rep. Nothing like it, experience-wise, so they tell me.'

'Well, that's fine, so long as the Inspector of Taxes can find it in his heart to be lenient.'

'That's no problem,' Kit said. 'It so happens that when Sarah and I got engaged she talked me into handing over all my financial business to Magnus's accountants. Everything I earn goes into some kind of fund, which they've made into a limited company. They take care of the tax side and I draw the same salary every month, whether I'm working or not. Of course they know every dodge in the book and in some fantastic way I seem to be much better off.'

'I shouldn't wonder. The only thing is . . .'

'What?'

'Doesn't it rather tie you to the family? I can see it would have been inevitable if you'd married, but do you really want to be stuck with them forever?'

He looked at me in a speculative way and then said with a touch of slyness:

'To be perfectly frank with you, darling, the same thought did flit through my tiny head, but it's not like that at all. I thrashed it out with Julie last night. She's really on the ball in some ways, and she explained that it's now passed right out of Magnus's hands. He simply set it up for me, and that was it. In fact, it's a joke to imagine that he'd have time for involvement in side issues of that kind. The financial outfit is completely autonomous, for a start.'

He went banging on in this strain for several minutes, boring me about the multiplicity and ramifications of the

Benson-Jones enterprises until I was tempted to repeat something which Magnus himself had told me about his attitude to details. However, it was not part of my plan to antagonise him and as soon as I could get a word in I said:

'So you've seen Julie? How is she?'

'Shattered, naturally. She'd hardly spent a day away from Sarah in her whole life. I think she'll pull out of it, though.'

'I imagine so, since she's already able to get steamed up over your financial affairs.'

'For God's sake, Tessa, don't be such a cat. It's not like that at all. The subject happened to come up and I asked her advice. It's as simple as that. I'm staying at the Hall, as of yesterday, if you must know.'

'Oh, I see.'

'I tried going back to the flat,' he said defensively, 'but it simply wasn't on. The press were lined up in wait half way down the street and the telephone never left off, day or night. Actually, it was Magnus who suggested I should go back to them till the heat's off. They have ways of keeping out of the glare.'

'I know, and as it happens, Kit, I'm really glad you're still in close touch, because there's something that's worrying me a bit.'

'You're not the only one.'

'This concerns Henry. Has anything been done about getting him a proper lawyer?'

'I wouldn't know.'

'Then do you think you could find out? Robin says the police will have explained to him that he's entitled to legal aid, and may even have put him on to a solicitor . . .'

'So what's your worry?'

'Well, you know as well as I do that they won't fall over themselves to see that he gets the best legal brains in the country, and anyway I doubt if he could afford it. Since Magnus is so keen on racial equality and fair do's all round, I thought he might be willing to pitch in.'

'You have a point there,' Kit agreed. 'It certainly wouldn't do his image any harm, would it? I'll have a word with Julie this evening.'

'Why not Magnus himself?'

'Because he's in Munich, or one of those. Won't be back till tomorrow night. And on the whole I'd rather do it through Julie. She has more . . . empathy.'

'Oh, has she? Well, thanks a lot. I'll leave it to you.'

He walked down the corridor with me as far as the back entrance to the car park, not forgetting to resume the grief-stricken expression for the benefit of the few people who scurried past us on their way out of the building. Irritated by this performance, I was stung into asking: 'By the way Kit, was it Julie or Magnus who persuaded you to try rep. instead of America?'

'Neither, for God's sake,' he answered in a blustering voice. 'What fantastic ideas you get hold of! You must be out of your mind.'

His tone was not exactly hostile, but it was not brimming over with empathy either, and I could only pray that my ill timed attempt to score off him had not done anything to jeopardise Henry's chances.

2

The answer was not long in coming. During the following day's lunch break, I was startled to find that Kit had come out of purdah and was already installed in the canteen, lunching with a celebrated journalist and broadcaster. He must have been positively bristling with empathy too, because Kit was giving him the full treatment of boyish grins and rueful headshakes. After about ten minutes they went out, still chatting, and I thought he had not noticed me, but in no time at all he was back again and sitting down at my table, where he promptly asked the waitress to bring him a brandy and soda.

'God, I needed that!' he said, setting down the half empty glass and plunging straight into the tensed up, teeth gritting act. 'Life can be pretty good hell sometimes.'

'As we can all now look forward to reading in our favourite newspaper,' I reminded him.

'The problem with you, my poor Tessa,' he informed me with weary resignation, 'is that you don't really have a clue about what being in the big time involves. I just hope you never have to learn the hard way, as I did. You needn't think I enjoyed that ordeal just now. It just so happens that the only answer, at this period of time, is to give one exclusive interview to someone you can be fairly confident won't crucify you, and tell the rest to go climb a tree.'

'Okay, I get the point, but you haven't bothered to come upstairs again just to give me the inside story of the price of fame, I take it?'

'Right. I came to tell you about Henry. It's not on.'

'Why not?'

'Magnus won't play. Julie says it's not that he's vindictive, but he won't lift a finger either way. So far as he's concerned, it's up to the jury to decide. I must say, I respect his attitude and, sentiment-wise, I find it totally viable.'

'In plain words, Magnus is behaving just like any conventional father?'

'Nothing wrong with that, is there?'

'No, except that I wouldn't have expected him to take quite such a predictable attitude. However, it just goes to show that even the most tolerant and magnanimous people are swayed by emotion when it comes to the crunch. He's back, is he?'

'Late last night. I didn't see him.'

'You didn't? Then how do you know what he feels about all this?'

'Much as I love you, sweetheart, I'm not prepared, even for your sake, to sit up until two in the morning waving your little banners for you with a full working day ahead of me.'

'I'm not asking you to, I simply wondered how it was you knew so much about the reception my little banner got?'

'I mentioned it to Julie, that's how. She stayed up for the Welcome Home bit, and she put it to him. And she got up again at six to have breakfast with me. So that's how I know. And it's now two o'clock, in case you're interested, and we're supposed to be back on the set.'

I said no more, but he reopened the subject when we had descended to the ground floor. Pausing outside the stage door, he said:

'I can't figure out what's in it for you, anyway, Tessa. Hopefully, he'll get a fair trial, and if they plead insanity I can see him spending a very comfortable little time in Broadmoor, or wherever. I'm sure he'll be allowed to run up a few bits of pottery, and maybe even play darts on his good days.'

He then leant his weight against the door and passed through it, not omitting to droop the shoulders in an attitude of quiet suffering as he stepped over the threshold. By gritting my teeth I just managed to restrain myself from pushing him flat on his beautiful, sad, complacent face.

CHAPTER TEN

1

Four days later and out of work, I paid a call on Gerald Pettigrew at his office in Essex Street. The premises of Barrett and Pettigrew being dreary and uninviting to a degree unparalleled even in the legal profession, I would have preferred some slightly more congenial surroundings in which to try and get my proposals across to him, but I had no choice. Gerald was paralysed from the waist down, as a result of being blown up in a battleship during the war, and was obliged to conduct all his business from a wheel chair.

Although physically such a wreck, his mind remained in tip top condition, and I knew that behind the bluff, rather naïf exterior, a shrewd brain was ticking away and that the innocent blue eyes looked out on the world with acute observation. I had frequently had reason to be grateful for his sound advice.

We had met just over a year before, through the death of a mutual friend, the one true love of poor Gerald's frustrated life, and ever since then I had made a point of disrupting his work from time to time and calling on him when I found myself in the neighbourhood. On this occasion, however, I had been at pains to assure him in advance that I was not to be regarded as a frivolous interruption, but as a bona fide client with a genuine legal problem. Henry had been brought before the Magistrates' Court and remanded in custody, pending his trial at the Oxford Assizes in approximately six weeks' time, and I had formed the opinion that not a minute of them should be lost.

When I had outlined the set up Gerald said:

'I read about the case, naturally. No one could avoid doing so. But I can't quite see what you expect your old Uncle Gerald to do about it.'

'I was hoping you might take him on. The first thing, obviously, is to fix him up with a good solicitor, who'll brief the right counsel and so on.'

'Now, hold on, old top! Those blighters cost a bomb. Even if I waived my fees, which I've no intention of doing, where's the rest of the lolly coming from?'

'Is that your only question, Gerald?'

'No, it isn't, not by a long chalk. Even a chump like you must realise that I can't go shoving my oar in uninvited. If the chap's got someone representing him there's nothing in the world I can do about it.'

'And that concludes your case for the opposition, does it?'

'Oh, I could probably rustle up a few more objections if I was pushed, but I should think that's enough to be going on with.'

'Well, it's not. In the first place, you can forget about the expense. I don't know how it will be raised, but I refuse to be bogged down by anything so stupid as money. As for your second point, there's no problem at all. Robin can easily wangle an interview with Henry. He'll ask if he'd like you to act for him and Henry will say yes and there we are.'

'Oh are we, by heck? That's all very fine, but how do you know he'll say anything of the kind? Robin being a policeman too, your pal Henry might well see it as just another move to tie the noose a bit tighter.'

'No, because I shall give Robin a letter, explaining that we're on his side and I think he'll believe me.'

'But are we, old horse? It sounds to me as though you'd got this very cut and dried in your own mind but I'll need a bit more than that before you drag me in. You haven't

produced one shred of evidence to show the fellow's innocent. I don't give a hoot for your personal opinion, and I
have a strong aversion to defending murderers, even when
I'm getting paid for it.'

'Well listen, Gerald, naturally I can't produce any proof.
If I could I wouldn't need you, would I? But in order to
convict someone you have to show beyond all reasonable
doubt that he did it, right?'

'That's the idea.'

'Well, I'm here to provide the reasonable doubt, that's
all; and I was hoping you'd listen to it.'

'And so I will, but let's get a few things straight first. Is
this just a character reference or have you got facts?'

'I think I have. To start with, I can name several people
with far stronger motives for wanting Sarah out of the way
than Henry had.'

Gerald leant back in his wheel chair and sighed deeply.
'Ah! I had a nasty feeling we were leading up to something
like that, and I must warn you that you're on a sticky wicket
there. Attempting to incriminate other people can be a bit
of a boomerang. It's more likely to harden opinion against
your friend than to get him off.'

'All right, drop that for now and consider the case as it
stands.'

'And you think you know what it consists of?'

'I know it's based on circumstantial evidence, for a start.
I was there when it happened, don't forget.'

'All the same, old horse, there are likely to be numerous things you don't know. People in this country don't get
arrested just on hearsay, not even if they're coloured, and I'm
beginning to suspect that's at the root of your partisanship.'

'To some extent you may be right, but it's not as simple
as that. I'm not suggesting that they've picked on Henry

for that reason alone, or that they would concoct evidence against him, or anything like that; and yet all the same the dice are loaded against him. I believe quite a lot of people would be relieved to see him convicted, not on account of his race, you know, but because he's an alien in a tight little community and they don't feel the same obligation to speak up on his behalf as they would for one of themselves. In other words, Gerald, I'm convinced there's a tacit conspiracy among a small group of people to withhold any information which might get Henry off the hook.'

'I wouldn't be at all surprised, but you'd have one hell of a job proving it. To return to our brass tacks, though; do you really know what this so-called circumstantial evidence consists of?'

'More or less. It begins before the crime was committed, when Sarah Benson-Jones had a brush with Henry and made him look rather silly in front of a crowd of about five hundred people. Revenge for that is supposed to have been his motive, combined with a slight mental confusion on his part, whereby he believed her to be a real witch, who had put the finger on him. Rather feeble, as you'll probably agree, but that's just one instance of his background counting against him. Another is that, owing to the social code he was brought up with, he has rather a reputation for not telling the truth. At least I've only heard that from one person, but as he went out of his way to tell me so, I presume that he's spread it around pretty thoroughly.'

'Anything to substantiate this argument that he believed himself to be under the spell of witchcraft?'

'Oh, you bet! No end of people are tumbling over themselves to point out that he was in a highly excitable mood. Since it was the first time in his life that he'd been to such a function and had walked away with every prize that was going, I personally can't see why he shouldn't have been feeling slightly elated, but Robin tells me that one witness actually described him as "trance-like" so you can tell from that which way the wind is blowing.'

'And what about you?'

'How do you mean?'

'How would you have described him? Be honest, for once in your miserable life.'

'Well, I'd be an idiot to pretend that he didn't look rather peculiar when he came out of the tent, but I can give you a perfectly rational explanation for that. If he'd waited inside for a few minutes, hoping Sarah would come back, and then got the urge to take a closer look at the tools of her trade, he couldn't have missed seeing her, lying there dead. It would have been enough to make anyone a bit jumpy.'

'And yet he denies having seen her? Wouldn't it have been more natural to come flying out and raise the alarm?'

'No, I should think it would have taken him about two seconds to realise the spot it would put him in. Most likely his instinct would be to keep quiet and get as far away as possible. It was just his bad luck that Babs and I happened to be waiting at the ringside. And, having kept quiet in the first place, he may have thought it would be even more damning to change his story afterwards. That's one of the ways in which I think a good lawyer might be able to advise him.'

'From what you've told me, it hardly sounds as though he needs advice. So far the case is non-existent but I presume there's more to come?'

'I'm afraid there is. His fingerprints were all over the dart, for one thing. Not that it has real significance because it wasn't the dart that killed her, and the knife which did hasn't even been found. But there's also the fact that he was carrying an enormous hold-all around with him, and that he was missing, or to put it another way no one admits having seen him during the forty minutes after he came out of the tent until the police had taken over and rounded everyone up for questioning.'

'That was a hell of a long time, surely? Did it really take them forty minutes?'

'Yes, owing to a series of misadventures, I'm afraid it did. There was a delay of at least twenty minutes before they were notified and the house is pretty isolated, you know; seven miles from the nearest town.'

'And where is Henry assumed to have been during all that time?'

'Please note that I didn't say he was missing; only that he wasn't seen; but it was a vast area and it could apply to dozens of people.'

'Except that, being of a somewhat distinctive appearance, he would have been harder to miss than most. However, I'll keep an open mind on that one, old girl. To repeat my question, what is he supposed to have been doing?'

'It is suggested that he was at the Missendale Potteries, which is about five miles away from Eglinton Hall.'

'He went by car?'

'Not unless he pinched one.'

'And obviously didn't thumb a lift, so that would appear to be a point in his favour. Ten miles on foot in forty minutes is pretty good going.'

I shook my head. There's a short cut through the fields, which lops off about half the distance, and furthermore Henry is no ordinary walker. He's in the marathon class. It's one more instance of his background counting against him.'

'Leaving that aside for a moment, what is supposed to have been the object of so much exercise? Not to dispose of the weapon, I take it?'

'No, to switch on the electric kiln. It had been out of action because of the holiday. Martin Graham says he turned it off on Thursday and had no reason to look at it again until Sunday morning when his other apprentice, a young man called Walter, passed the remark that it was rather wasteful to keep it running at full tilt all through the weekend.'

'How long does it take to heat up?'

'About five hours. Which means that anyone at all could have switched it on during Saturday morning. Anyone, that is, except this very Walter, who had left to spend the night with a friend in Oxford. It could also have been done on Saturday evening by anyone at all, including Walter, but the police don't favour either of these possibilities.'

'Why not?'

'Because of something Mrs Graham told them. They'd asked her to pack an overnight case for Henry and take it to the police station. She got home at about seven o'clock and in order to reach the students' quarters, which are in a kind of Nissen hut at the back, she had to pass this kiln and she noticed it was firing. She says that it didn't occur to her that there was anything wrong in that because she knew that her husband had a heap of stuff to finish off for an exhibition next week at the local crafts museum; but nevertheless she was curious enough to look at the thermometer and she says it was registering at about half way. In which case it must have been switched on at some time between four and six that afternoon.'

'From the way you report it, I get a hint that Mrs Graham may not have been speaking the truth?'

'I honestly don't know, Gerald, but it's like I told you. There are so many odds and ends and when you put them together they do add up to something rather formidable. On the other hand, if only one person is lying, the whole lot might collapse. What worries me is that I think they're ganging up. Not from malice, necessarily, but because they're afraid of the truth coming out, and Henry makes a convenient scapegoat. I haven't told you the last bit.'

'Spit it out then, old girl.'

'It's just as damning and just as nebulous as all the rest. The police naturally got in a twitter of excitement over the kiln and as soon as it was cool enough to go inside they removed what ashes there were for analysis. They included some rusty looking metal objects, which turned out to be the buttons off one of the students' overalls. So what have you got? The answer to the last little teasing question of why there were no bloodstains on Henry's clothes when he came out of the tent.'

Gerald frowned: 'Hang on a sec., I'm not quite with you. Do you imply that he'd taken his overall to the party?'

'Stowed away in the hold-all.'

'Then I don't get it. From what you'd told me, I thought this was alleged to be an unpremeditated job. Otherwise the motive goes up in smoke. If he'd come prepared, he must have planned the deed in advance?'

I shook my head. 'It's not as easy as that. You see, the Pottery had its own display at the fête. Some of the stuff was on sale and, as a kind of gimmick, they'd set up a wheel and were charging people twenty-five pence to have a go on it. The customer was given a lump of clay and allowed to keep the finished article. During the lulls a professional pot thrower, either Martin or one of his trainees, would give an expert demonstration, to fool the public into thinking how easy it was. It didn't work out as planned because Henry became so infatuated with all the other side shows that he rather let the side down, and Walter the other boy, was even worse. He didn't show up at all until about five o'clock.

But the point is that Henry had a perfectly valid reason for bringing his overall and you could argue that he only got the idea later of using it for a more sinister purpose.'

'I see,' Gerald said, slowly swivelling his wheel chair round in a complete circle. When he was facing me again he seemed to have come to a decision, for he asked me: 'Do you happen to know the name of the solicitors who are acting for him?'

'Some local firm, I believe. I could get Robin to find out. Does that mean you're going to take a hand?'

'Shouldn't think so for a moment, but I'd be interested to know what line the defence means to take.'

'Oh Gerald, you are a love! Thank you so much.'

Being the most sentimental old solicitor who ever breathed, he immediately turned bright scarlet and commanded me to put a sock in it, although he managed to resume the mantle of the steely hearted lawyer before we parted.

'I haven't promised anything, mind!' he called out as I was leaving the room.

'No, Gerald.'

'I'll look into it and give you a buzz in a day or two. That's all I'm saying.'

'It's all I want.'

'And another thing!'

'Yes?'

'I know that I'd be better off talking to a brick wall, but I'd watch my step, if I were you. Drop this idea of trying to find someone else to pin it on. You might live to regret it. If you're right in thinking Henry innocent, the real culprit could be quite a ruthless customer.'

'I agree with you entirely,' I said. 'Which is why I need your help.'

2

The faint qualms which Gerald's final warning had aroused were soon smothered by the reflection that it had doubtless been issued purely as a matter of form. Clearly, the most efficient way to cut through the net round Henry was to wrap the real murderer in an even tighter one, and the only remaining problem was how to set about it. Having pondered the matter for about twenty minutes on the return journey to Beacon Square, I decided that the first move must be to insinuate myself once more into Eglinton Hall, and that the surest route to it lay through Julie. This presented me with the necessity of inventing some plausible excuse for ringing her up and although one or two vague solutions had occurred to me the drive was over before I had hit on one which measured up to all requirements.

It was therefore in the nature of a pat on the back from my guardian angel to find a message on the hall table, stating that Miss Benson-Jones had telephoned and wished me to call her back. I lost no time in doing so and she answered in person.

'Kit mentioned that you wouldn't be working this week,' she began, 'and I was wondering if we could meet? There's something I'd like to talk over with you, if you could spare me an hour or two. I'd ask you out to lunch, but I have to avoid public places at present. Would it be a nuisance to come and see you at home?'

She had knocked over so many of the anticipated obstacles with this speech, which came out very pat and yet at the same time flat and breathless, as though over-rehearsed, that I began to regret not having spent more time charting the open sea before pushing the boat out. Catching up as fast as I could, I said:

'Not a nuisance at all, Julie, I'd be delighted. The only snag is that I'd planned to be away for a few days. Robin has to go abroad again and since I'm out of work it seemed a good chance. I could put it off, I suppose . . .'

'Oh no, certainly not,' she cut in, sounding stiff and formal, and convinced that it was now she who was faced with the unforeseen hitch, I made haste to sweep it aside.

'Oh, wait though, Julie! I've just remembered something. Listen, I'm only going to stay with my cousin Toby. You remember him? Well, he lives quite near you, at Roakes Common, and I shan't be tied down to any programme while I'm there. Why don't we meet for lunch at Dedley, or somewhere?'

This was the real hurdle, and it was as much as I could do to hold on to the reins while she considered the proposal. I was thankful for my restraint, however, because extra persuasion might have put her on her guard and as it was she took only thirty seconds to come up with the right answer. It was agreed that I should lunch with her at Eglinton Hall on the following Wednesday.

I was so elated by the ease with which all this had been accomplished that I almost forgot to telephone Toby and warn him that I was coming.

CHAPTER ELEVEN

1

MAGNUS was out when I arrived on Wednesday morning, and Julie explained that he was playing golf.

'I rather pushed him into it,' she admitted. 'He's not used to going on his own, but it's so bad for him not to have regular exercise. He used to play a lot with Sarah, you know.

She was a marvellous player, quite often used to beat him. Nothing is the same without her,' she added dismally, looking down at her deformed foot as though literally to point to her own inadequacy.

'Yes, I can imagine how dreadfully you must miss her,' I agreed. 'You especially. Somehow or other, men seem to have more sides to their life than women.'

'How right you are, Tessa! I hadn't thought of it but I suppose it does give them a better perspective. And you know Magnus was far more adjusted than I was to the prospect of Sarah's marriage. I can admit that now and, ironically enough, I can see that I shouldn't be suffering half so badly if only I'd reconciled myself to it.'

'Oh, I doubt that,' I told her. 'One can never be wholly prepared for losing someone, however much you try to adapt to it in advance. Perhaps if Sarah had married years ago and had been living far away when she died you wouldn't have felt it so intensely, but that's a state of mind which creeps up on you gradually. You can't push yourself into it and you and Sarah were so particularly close, weren't you? It seemed to me that you drew everything from each other.'

'How understanding you are!' she murmured, her great dark eyes swimming with tears. 'And everything you say is so true. Do you know, Sarah and I always had our clothes made exactly alike? It sounds absurd, I expect, but I can't imagine ever buying anything new for myself now. And we shared a bedroom all our lives. Some people found that rather strange, Babs laughed about it quite openly, but it always seemed perfectly natural to us.'

She relapsed into silent contemplation of these memories, and I was wondering whether it would be tactless to ask her what she had wanted to see me about when she said:

'I hardly dare ask this, but would you . . . could you consider . . . ?'

'What?'

'Coming to stay here for a few days? While your husband's away, I mean? I realise it's asking a lot, but Magnus has to go abroad again soon and I dread the thought of being entirely on my own. I wouldn't impose on you, I promise. You'd be absolutely free to come and go as you pleased. But you're so sensible, as well as sympathetic, and just knowing you were in the house and that I could turn to you if things got unbearable would be such a comfort. I suppose you think that's a lot to ask?'

'No, I don't, but there must be someone better fitted than me. Haven't you some close friend you could invite?'

'No, I haven't, not one. I know it must sound odd, but Sarah and I were self sufficient you see. We never went away to school because of my illness and her not wanting to leave me. And somehow being very rich does cut one off from other people, in a way. I have dozens of acquaintances but not a single real friend. I've never needed one till now.'

'How about family? Cousins and so on?'

'None of those either. Magnus never speaks much about his childhood, but I believe his parents died before he grew up. I don't even know whether he had brothers and sisters, but it must be years since he had any communication with them. And it was the same with my mother, in a way. Her family cut her off completely when she married. I'm not sure why, but she came from a much grander background than Magnus, so perhaps it was pure snobbery. He wasn't nearly so well off and successful in those days.'

'But when she died didn't they make any sort of move towards a reconciliation with you and Sarah?'

'Not that I remember. We were in Beirut, you know, so there was probably no question of their coming out for the funeral; and I was so ill myself at the time. In fact, there's a whole year out of my life when I could just as well have been dead too. And afterwards there was just Sarah. Magnus flitted in and out of our lives, but mainly it was just the two of us. So, you see, now that she's gone I don't really belong anywhere.'

It was a forlorn little speech, and to cheer her up I said: 'I'll try my best, Julie, but I'll have to find out what Robin's plans are before I can give you an answer.'

She thanked me with such fervour that I felt rather a fraud and very nearly waived the conditions and accepted her invitation on the spot.

The big advantage of Magnus's absence, from my point of view was that Julie and I were not required to face each other down the length of the refectory table. Lunch was served to us in front of the drawing room fire.

'Have you seen Kit lately?' she asked me in a fluting hostessy tone, reminiscent of Sarah's best, and presumably for the benefit of the butler who was busying himself at our side.

'No, not since we finished shooting. Well, I couldn't have, come to think of it, seeing he's abroad.'

'Abroad?' she repeated in a stunned voice then recovering herself went on: 'Oh yes, how silly of me! I just thought you might have seen him before he left?'

'Well no, there was hardly time. He was spending the weekend in Rome, before going on to Paris on Monday. Or did he change his mind about that?' I asked, doing my best for her.

'I don't think so. Let me see, it was Monday he had to be in Paris, was it?'

'Monday or Tuesday. His film is opening with a rattle of drums on the Champs Elysées tonight, and they wanted him for a p.a.,' I reminded her.

'Yes, of course. The fact is, I get so confused with dates just now.'

'Which is quite understandable.'

Having emerged from this brief skirmish relatively unscathed, we picked away at the shrimps in our avocados for a bit, and then she said:

'The reason why I asked if you'd seen him was because of something we were talking about just before he went away. It was to do with Henry.'

'You mean about getting him a lawyer? Don't worry, he reported back on that. So far as you're concerned, the subject is closed.'

'How do you mean, so far as I'm concerned?' she asked sharply.

Before I could answer the door opened again and the butler rolled in a trolley loaded with a fresh batch of silver dishes. A fairly elaborate performance of swopping around of plates and doling out of escalopes then took place and when he had retired again Julie said:

'Could you repeat exactly what Kit told you?'

'Certainly. He said it was no go.'

'But did he explain why?'

'Honestly, Julie, is this why you wanted to see me? If so, please relax. Kit made your father's attitude quite clear. I accept it and I understand, so the matter is closed.'

'Then you do know it was his decision and not mine?'

'Why yes, it never occurred to me that it wasn't,' I replied, the contrary now occurring to me for the first time. 'And you couldn't go against his wishes in a thing like that, whatever your private views were.'

'No.'

'So there's no more to be said.'

She ran her finger round the rim of her glass, staring down at it, so that I could not see her face, and began to speak in a slow, monotonous voice.

'It was just that . . . well, I supposed what bothered me was that you seemed to give in too easily. I'm a fairly observant person, I believe. I've had to spend so much of my life watching from the sidelines that it's become a habit. Somehow, I'd expected a bit more resistance on your part.'

'And that's why you invited me to lunch? To find out whether I had given up or not?'

'Partly. You see, I didn't hear a word from Kit after we'd discussed it. I tried ringing him, but there was no reply. It was stupid of me, but I'd forgotten all about the Paris trip. I was afraid he might have given you the wrong impression.'

'How could he have done that?'

'By letting you think it was my wish that there should be no . . . interference in the trial and so on. I just thought, if that were so, you might still feel justified in going ahead, but that if you knew the decision had come from Magnus it would make all the difference.'

One thing you can say for the onlookers of life is that when they do enter the game they are apt to run on with rather less subtlety than the more experienced players who usually prefer to keep something in reserve. Being in no hurry to take the ball away from her, I said:

'But are you telling me that no one is allowed to lift a finger to help Henry simply because your father has vetoed it?'

Some extra pressure of her finger caused the glass to tilt forward, and she had to pull it back hastily to stop the wine from spilling out.

'So I was right,' she said in a tight voice. 'You do intend to go on with it?'

'I didn't exactly say that. And, after all, even the smartest lawyer on earth probably couldn't get Henry off if he's guilty. Unfortunately the converse is equally true.'

'I thought it was a matter for the judge and jury to decide?'

'Listen, Julie, why not come straight out with it? You don't give a damn what happens, so long as Henry gets convicted, isn't that true?'

'Yes, it is, in a way, because I happen to believe he's guilty. There simply isn't any alternative. No one who knew Sarah could have done such a dreadful thing, and if it was an outsider it has to be Henry. It's as simple as that.'

'As Kit would say. So you've nothing to fear, have you? If you're right, the best lawyer in the world couldn't get him off.'

'I know that. What bothers me is that all sorts of facts which have no direct bearing on the case might come to light, simply because an unscrupulous counsel wouldn't hesitate to use them, however painful they might be for other people. Obviously, he'd start by delving into Sarah's past, looking for alternative motives and so on.'

'And you're positive he wouldn't find any, so what have you got to lose?'

'To put it rather dramatically, my sister's good name.'

'Oh!'

'I hadn't meant to tell you, because I'm now the only living soul who knows. The secret ought to have been safe, but you've forced my hand.'

'Well, I'm sorry about that, Julie, but you've really no obligation to tell me, or anyone else for that matter; unless of course it's something which would clear Henry, in which case I suppose even you would feel compelled to?'

'It wouldn't clear him; quite the reverse. In fact, it gives him a stronger motive than anyone has guessed, but when I said I was the only person who knew about it, that wasn't quite true. Henry knows, and what terrifies me is that the defence might get it out of him and use it to prove intense provocation, or whatever the legal phrase is. You see, about six months ago, before she met Kit, Sarah had an affair with Henry.'

'I don't believe it!'

'I swear. It didn't last long, and she wasn't in love with him, but he has this odd kind of magnetism, which you remarked on yourself. Of course the attraction soon wore off. It was wrong in every way. I don't mean because he was coloured, please don't think that, but he was years younger than her and they hadn't a single interest in common. It was Sarah who broke it off, and you can see that might be used to suggest that she led him on, and then dropped him when he ceased to amuse her?'

'Did she tell you about it?'

'She denied it at first . . . but I knew there was someone. She was bitterly ashamed of it by then. Luckily, soon after that Kit came into our lives.'

Noting the plural, I said:

'How did she meet him?'

'Through me, oddly enough. I have to go to a hospital near Aylesbury every few months for check ups and therapy. I usually stay in for three or four days and it never does the slightest good, but Sarah insisted on my keeping up with it. She used to drive me there and collect me herself, to make sure I didn't back out, I expect. Anyway, about six months ago, when I was due to come home, Kit came round on one of those goodwill tours his press agent had fixed up and we talked for a bit. When he found out where I lived he said it was practically on his way and he could drop me off. So I rang Sarah and told her I was getting a lift. Of course she wanted to know who with, and then she made me invite him to dinner, and that was how it all began.'

'To get back to Henry, though, so long as he doesn't say anything, no one can force you to . . .'

She raised her hand in a warning gesture, at the same time turning her head towards the door.

'I think I hear Magnus,' she said, looking more scared than the circumstances warranted. 'For God's sake, Tessa, don't say a word about this to him, I implore you.'

She stood up, turning away from me and squaring her shoulders. Then, with head high and face wreathed in radiant smiles, she stepped forward to greet her father. The movement and expression were such a grotesque travesty of Sarah's that I wondered Magnus could bear to look at her without bursting into tears or laughter; but then I saw that the act had been lost on him and that he had eyes only for his companion. Simultaneously Julie realised it too and shrank back into her normal diffident and crooked stance as Babs Graham, aglow in pastel tweeds, wafted triumphantly across the room.

2

'Tell me something,' I said. 'You're a man of the world, or have been in your time; would you have described Sarah Benson-Jones as a nymphomaniac?'

'I am not a man of that world,' Toby answered coldly. 'And she didn't pester me with disagreeable proposals, if that's what you mean?'

'Not exactly, but sometimes men have an insight into these things; so Robin tells me.'

'Then he is the one you should ask.'

'How can I, when he never met her? Anyway, if you can't give me a snap judgement try a considered one based on the facts.'

'What are they?'

'That up until her death Sarah was engaged to Kit but, according to Julie, she'd only just climbed out of Henry's bed when they met.'

'You startle me! However, perhaps nymphomania is too strong a word?'

'Yes, but there have also been hints of something between her and Walter. Now, since all these three were unknown to her until about six months ago, you could at least say she was a fast worker. And these are only the names we've heard about. There could well be others and if so doesn't it open up all sorts of fresh possibilities about motives and so on? Supposing, for the sake of argument, that she'd also had a go with Martin? How would Babs have cared for that?'

'I imagine she'd have been highly delighted. Since you tell me she's busily cantering after Sir Mag, it would probably have suited her ideally. However, Sarah didn't strike me particularly in that way. Bumptious and boring, I agree, but not over-sexed. In fact, her weakness was more likely in promising more than she meant to fulfil. The other one is much more the type.'

'Which other one? Babs?'

'Don't be silly. Babs is far too calculating to throw her bonnet about. I mean the sister. Those repressed, intense young women often turn out to be the most tiresome little Jezebels at heart.'

'Are you serious, Toby, or just trying to put me off?'

'I'm not so optimistic.'

'And you really mean it about Julie? I wonder if you're right? It would be a much more logical reason for wanting to hush it up. She might rely on Henry holding his tongue, since it had no bearing on the murder, but if a clever lawyer were to get at him, the whole story would be liable to come out. He could even subpoena Julie as a witness.'

'I don't see why he should. As you've said, it has no relevance.'

'Ah, but what if Sarah had found out and, under cover of telling Henry's fortune, had warned him off, or maybe threatened him? How does that strike you?'

'Only as a glancing blow, since you assure me he's innocent.'

'Yes, that's true, but it might tie in somehow. Anyway, I'm really getting sold on this idea that it was Julie and not Sarah. Julie is the world's foremost liar, as it happens.' Toby sighed: 'I can't keep pace with you. Last time we discussed her you stated the exact opposite.'

'I know, but that was because she made such a botch of pretending it wasn't Walter who nearly killed us on his motor bike. She must have been off form then, but she excelled herself at lunch today. The fact is that everything she told me was based on a complete falsehood.'

'Fancy!'

'It was, you know. She began by impressing on me that the refusal to help Henry came directly from her father, hinting that she, personally, didn't go along with it.'

'So?'

'So why does she then give me what is supposed to be the reason for hushing things up and insist at the same time that she's the only one, apart from Henry, who knows about it? Either her father knows too, or he doesn't. And if he doesn't, the decision not to help Henry probably didn't come from him at all.'

'Meaning that she quoted him without bothering to consult him?'

'Exactly. And I can tell you that she nearly had a fit when he returned unexpectedly while we were discussing it. Obviously she was scared stiff that I would leap forward and say that I quite understood his feelings about the trial and so on, and he wouldn't have had the faintest idea what I was talking about. Well, it makes sense of a kind, but I do wish I knew for certain. It makes everything doubly difficult to be working in the dark.'

'Perhaps Babs could shed a little light?'

'What makes you think so?'

'I don't know, but it sounds as though she's making a better job of stepping into Sarah's shoes than the other creature. Perhaps she's in Mag's confidence?'

I considered this. 'Yes, I daresay a lot of Julie's behaviour arises from false hopes of taking Sarah's place; and she looked like bringing it off at first. She was the one who kept her head and gave out orders when Sarah was killed. Magnus was putty in her hands at that point, and Kit too. He became utterly dependent on Julie for a while, but that didn't last either. As soon as he was back on his feet again and the nasty policemen had gone away, he went trotting off to Rome without even bothering to let her know. One sees now that it was just a flash in the pan for poor old Julie. She's right back where she's always been, lady-in-waiting to the reigning queen.'

'And not even related to the current one, which must be so galling for her.'

'She'll be more galled than ever when they are related, which is presumably what Babs is after. Do you know that Julie actually tried to sell me the idea that she had to bully Magnus into playing golf this morning? That's a laugh if you like. When they came back it was perfectly obvious that the whole thing had been fixed up between him and Babs. He's giving her lessons, it appears.'

'Oh, not that tired old gambit?'

'Why not? Women like Babs always use the tired old gambits and men like Magnus always fall for them. I believe you're right. Babs is the key and I must find a way of manipulating her to unlock a few mysteries. Now, how shall I set about it, Toby? Oh, I know.'

'So soon?'

'Yes, it's occurred to me that Robin's got this rather bright nephew who's leaving school and wants to take up potting. You know the one I mean? He's frightfully good looking and loaded with money. I am sure Babs could give us a few tips.'

'And something has occurred to me too,' Toby remarked.

'What?'

'Being such a dealer in the tired old gambits, she may recognise one when it rears up and slaps her between the eyes. Can't you think of something more original?'

'Not offhand. Can you?'

'Oh, I shouldn't dream of entering your foolish game. If Babsie is the murderer, which wouldn't surprise me at all, I don't want to have anything to do with her, and I think you'd be well advised to follow my example.'

'Yes, I know, Toby, but unfortunately it's not in my nature to play safe. Besides, one has to think of Henry. You haven't met him, but he has a quality about him, a kind of indolence, really, which doesn't go with high passions and violence. I can't get it out of my head that someone, somehow, has faked the evidence, and if I don't do something about it, I don't know who else will. I have a nasty feeling that even Gerald doesn't take me very seriously.'

'Well, I won't argue. You are free, white and twenty-one, as they were so fond of saying in my youth.'

'Unlike Henry,' I reminded him.

CHAPTER TWELVE

1

THE most direct route from Roakes Common to Missendale lay through the village of Eglinton but since this involved certain potential hazards which I could well do without, I mapped out a wide detour round to the north, whereby to approach my destination from the opposite direction.

During the first part of the drive I applied myself to putting some flesh on the bones of Robin's mythical nephew, but failed to make a convincing job of it, being constantly obliged to break the thread in order to check on my where-abouts. Very few of the villages I had so carefully listed actually figured on the signposts, and those that did had a whimsical habit of vanishing again whenever I came to a crossroads. Twice I had to turn round and go back on my tracks and finally I gave up altogether and stopped at a hamlet to ask for directions. It consisted of one shop and half a dozen houses, but contained the usual high proportion of deaf mutes and recent arrivals from Outer Mongolia, and the depressing outcome was that I eventually found myself bowling along the very road I had been at such pains to avoid. The suspicion was finally confirmed when I saw, just ahead of me, the inn sign of the *Eglinton Arms*. However, at least I was sure of my way from this point and as I slowed to a crawl, before making the sharp left turn into the lane, I felt reasonably confident that my presence in the danger area had not been observed.

Nevertheless, there was one most unfortunate sidekick to all this deliberate and unintentional circumnavigation, for I was now faced with the prospect of arriving at the Potteries at about ten minutes to two, which was really no time to drop in to discuss the career of even the most loaded and beautiful of nephews. There was nothing for it but to put him into cold storage while I worked out some emergency measures and, estimating that I was within a mile or so of my objective, I stopped the car on a straight, deserted stretch of road and got out to attend to the nearside back wheel.

The roar of an engine approaching at speed caused me to straighten up again in a hurry, just in time to see a motor cycle go hurtling past, in the same direction as myself and missing my offside wing by a couple of centimetres. This gave rise to some rather disturbing speculations and I was half tempted to drop the quest and turn for home, but a little reflection assured me that, even if I had been recognised, I could just as well have been examining the tyre's defect as creating it. Moreover, I no longer had much choice. A last bedraggled limp to the Potteries was about the most that could be expected of a tyre that had already had half the air let out of it.

All was silent and deserted when I arrived, and repeated knocks and rings brought no response. Feeling as deflated as the tyre, I was about to turn away when the door was flung open by Walter. He was at his most truculent and informed me curtly that neither of the Grahams was at home.

'Any idea when they'll be back?'

'Nope. Mr Graham's over at the museum, fixing up about the exhibition. B'lieve Mrs Graham meant to drop him off and go on to the golf club. All I know is they were to be back here by one and not a sign.'

'But that probably means they'll be home any time now?'

'No telling. Mr Graham is liable to skip meals when he gets stuck into something like this. Wouldn't bother to wait, if it was me.'

He was wearing his motor cycling gear, with gloves sticking out of the pockets, but his leather jacket was unbuttoned and the straps of his helmet hanging loose and I said:

'Are you going out, or coming in?'

'Going out. I'm supposed to be in charge here till they get back, but you get to feeling hungry after a while. Thought I'd take myself down for a snack at the pub.'

'Well, I don't want to stop you, but do you happen to know whether there's a pump on the premises?'

'What kinda pump?'

'The kind that pumps things up. I've got a flat tyre. It's probably a slow puncture, but it might get me home all right if we could just put some air in it.'

'Let's go take a look,' he said, emerging on to the doorstep, and then rather surprisingly slamming the door behind him and pocketing the key.

'It doesn't seem to have got any worse,' I admitted, as we stood gazing down at the tyre.

'Could be a slow puncture,' he said, with the solemnity of a surgeon making rather a horrid diagnosis. 'Best thing might be to leave it awhile and see if it goes down any more. Feel like joining me for a bit to eat?'

'On your pillion?'

'Well, why not, at that?' he asked, staring at me in an oddly speculative way.

I was tempted to accept, for I was feeling hungry myself, but there was a shiftiness in his manner, suggesting that his invitation sprang mainly from a desire to get me off the premises, even at the cost of being, literally, saddled with me. On the whole, I considered that my best chance of discovering what lay behind this scheme was by thwarting it. Gambling on his not being so unchivalrous as to leave me standing in the road, I said:

'Thanks, but I really should be on my way. My cousin's expecting me. Are you sure there isn't a pump somewhere?'

'Not that I know of,' he replied, and then, as though reluctantly bowing to the inevitable, he gave the tyre a smart kick, saying: 'You gotta jack?'

'In the boot. I'm not quite sure how to use it though.'

'Shouldn't take long to find out. How about the spare?'

'Yes, there's one of those too.'

'Okay, I'll change the wheel for you.'

'Oh, Walter, you are kind! What about your lunch though?'

'Only take a minute. Nothing to it,' he replied, with the quiet confidence of the expert.

Nevertheless, he made fairly heavy weather over it, examining each tool in turn and whistling through his teeth, in evident disapproval of its design and manufacture. After several abortive attempts to get the jack into position I diffidently suggested consulting the handbook, but he waved this amateurish suggestion aside, and finally removed his helmet, lay down on his back and wriggled headfirst underneath the car, dragging the jack after him. No further conversation was permissible and as it had occurred to me that the spare tyre was also likely to need some air, I seized the chance to make a personal inspection of the garage.

I did not find a pump, which proves nothing, for I barely had time to scratch the surface. Although the door was shut, it was not locked, but I had to squeeze my way very carefully into the interior, because practically the whole space was taken up by a shabby, mud splattered Ford Cortina, and any incautious movement would have sent me rubbing up against either it or the equally grimy garage wall. It was vaguely surprising to find that people who lived in such down-at-heel style as the Grahams should own two cars, particularly as this was such a demonstrable one-car garage, but my thoughts were chiefly concerned with picking my way forward with the right mixture of agility and caution, and it was not until I was about half way between the entrance and the end wall that a fresh surprise caused me to undo all the good work by reeling sideways against the wall.

I was on a level with the car's rear door by this time and my eye had been caught by a vivid patch of pink and yellow tweed. When I dared a second look, I saw that Babs was leaning forward over the steering wheel. It was an unlikely spot to have chosen for a siesta, and remembering all the tales I had heard about people being asphyxiated by exhaust fumes, I nerved myself to move forward again and place a hand on the bonnet. It was quite cold, but the movement had naturally brought me within close-up view of the figure in the driving seat, and I opened my mouth to let out a piercing yell. The extraordinary thing was that the piercing yell which simultaneously rent the air came not from me at all, but from outside the garage. Rigid with terror, I just managed to turn my head in the direction of the sound and saw Walter standing in the doorway:

'Hey!' he bellowed. 'What goes on? You in there, Mrs Price?'

Panic having now subsided a little, I scraped and bumped my way towards him. His face was distorted with rage, which I vaguely attributed to my having wandered off without permission, but it was no time for explanations and I said:

'Walter, I'm afraid something has happened to Mrs Graham. Did you know . . . ?' then broke off as I realised that he was not listening to me, but staring in a demented fashion into the alleyway which separated the garage from the house. This was a narrow path, overgrown with nettles and made even dingier by the fact that the light at the far end was partially blocked by a line of washing hanging out to dry. Apart from that, there was nothing to be seen except a pair of battered and rusty dustbins, so choked with rubbish that their lids sat rakishly askew and some of the mess had overflowed on to the ground. It was a squalid sight, but I could see nothing to arouse such frenzied emotions, until Walter rounded on me, saying in a high pitched, tremulous voice:

'Where the hell's my bike gone?'

'I've no idea; but listen to me a moment, Walter, please!'

'What? Oh, okay, but when I get my hands on the bastard who's taken it—you sure you didn't see anyone?'

'No, I didn't, and for heaven's sake stop going on about it. I'm trying to tell you that Mrs Graham's in there, and I think she must be ill, or she's passed out, or . . . anyway, you've got to come and see.'

His rage subsided and the high colour drained from his face as he took it in at last.

'In the garage? How could she be?'

'That's what we have to find out. Maybe she's only fainted, but I don't think so, and you must come and help me.'

'You must be crazy,' he mumbled, trailing reluctantly after me. 'What would she be doing in there?'

This time I continued on past the driver's door, barely glancing inside to confirm that the figure slumped over the wheel had not moved, and then waited for Walter to catch up with me. He, meanwhile, had seen her too and had collapsed against the car, his face the colour of wet clay and his adam's apple gyrating violently.

'You'd better get the door open. There may still be something we can do for her,' I told him though reconciled, even as I spoke, to the fact that this was asking too much of him.

I waited with diminishing hope, then gritted my teeth and wrenched the door open myself. The movement caused the body of the car to swing a little, dislodging the other body inside, so that it slithered sideways and I had to ram the door shut again, to prevent it sliding halfway out of the car. I was just fast enough to avert this particular horror, but something else had slid through the gap and stopped the door from closing completely. It was a steel shafted golf club, with a piece of paper, covered in red scrawls, wrapped round the leather hand grip.

Had I been alone I might have been tempted to pull it off and read the message and could just as well have done so for when I turned round I found that Walter had flopped on to the ground in a dead faint. So I was on my own again and there were more urgent matters to attend to than catching up with the latest bulletin from the Clean Up Britain Crusade.

I found a garden spade hanging from a nail on the garage wall, and by jamming the blade into the ground and propping the handle against the car door, I managed to hold it in place. When I was satisfied that it was secure, I bent down and groped in Walter's pocket for the front door key, then picked my way over his recumbent form and let myself into the house to look for a telephone.

2

There was nothing of the slow-speaking, burly British Bobby about Dedley's Chief Inspector Arnold Payne. In fact Nature, with a little help from his tailor, had designed him for the exactly opposite role and if he had walked into the Studio casting office and applied for the part of the chief crook, I feel certain he would have got it on the spot, possibly at gun point.

He was a sharp-eyed, sinister looking man, with black sideburns running down to his jaw. He also had a very low forehead and this, combined with a trick of shooting up his heavy black eyebrows in an exaggerated expression of astonishment, gave me the idea that I might eventually produce something so startling in the way of evidence that the hair and eyebrows would finally make contact. Curiously enough, this unusual appearance in one of his calling was distinctly reassuring, conveying the suggestion that even the wiliest criminal would need to get up fairly early in the morning to put anything across Arnold.

The fact that he was an old mate of Robin's, although senior to him in age and rank, also helped things along and the seal was put on our friendship by the revelation that he was an ardent movie fan. How far these favourable winds contributed to the closing of the credibility gap I cannot tell, but he listened in sympathetic silence to the tale of my journey to Missendale and all that had followed from it, and, so far as I know, no attempt was made then or later to verify it. In fact, he complimented me on the pertinence and brevity of my statement.

No such tribute could be paid to Walter. On returning to the garage, after notifying the police, I had found him on his feet again, though still groggy, and presumably the sight of me revived all the shocking memories, for a terrified look sprang into his eyes and he covered them with his hands and leant against the boot of the car while I was speaking to him.

'Try and get a grip, Walter. The police are on their way but one of us had better stand guard here until they arrive. Any idea how we could find Mr Graham?'

He shook his head, neither speaking nor uncovering his face.

'Oh, do try and be sensible, Walter! You must see that he ought to be told, preferably before the police get to him. Doesn't the museum have a telephone?'

He still did not answer and, not even sure that he had heard me, I was about to try again when he said in a muffled voice,

'Whassa time?'

'Ten past two. Why?'

'Then we won't be able to reach him. The museum is closed between one and three.'

'Oh, never mind that. It may be closed to the public, but there must be someone in charge. If you don't know the number, just tell me the name and I'll probably find it in the book.'

My brisk tones were finally having an effect, for he now looked up at me, saying quite calmly:

'Yes, you're right, Mrs Price. Sorry to be dim. It just knocked me out for a while, but I guess I can find the number. There's a card in the office. Would you be okay on your own here, if I was to deal with that end?'

It was not quite the arrangement I would have chosen, but in my relief at seeing him function again I was prepared to fall in with it.

'Yes, but have you thought what you'll say to him?'

'Just that there's been an accident. Isn't that right?'

'As far as it goes, but he'll want more than that.'

'Then I'll have to play it by ear. Don't worry, Mrs Price, I know him a whole lot better than you do, and this is really my job.'

He had become commendably sane and responsible all of a sudden and, watching him walk away, I congratulated myself on my tactful handling. It was not until almost an hour later that it dawned on me that I had just perpetrated one of the stupidest actions of my life.

3

'Oh yes, and what message would that be?' the chief inspector asked during his second and more detailed interrogation. We were on such a comfortable footing by this time that I had ventured to put a question of my own.

'The one wrapped round the handle of the golf club. You must have noticed it, surely?'

My voice faltered as his forehead contracted to a narrow white stripe and he waited for me to continue:

'I presume she was killed with the golf club?'

'Yes, that seems likely.'

'Then you must have examined it pretty thoroughly and you can't have missed the paper. Do you mean there was no writing on it?'

I would not say that his manner had become at all hostile but a certain reserve had crept in, and in one stroke we had moved into the realm of interrogator and witness, and not such a bright witness at that.

'Well now, Mrs Price, you've been most helpful, but naturally it was a shock, and it's not surprising if you've become a little confused. Not to worry, it's a perfectly normal reaction.'

'No, I promise you, inspector, it's not like that at all. I admit it was a shock, but it wasn't my first experience of that kind, and I hardly knew Mrs Graham, so there are no emotional complications. There really was a piece of paper attached to the golf club, and I really do believe it could be important.'

'Fair enough! And I'll tell you what we'll do. You run along and put your feet up in the other room, and I'll get someone to bring you a cup of tea. We'll need your finger-prints, just for elimination you understand, and while that's being done I'll have a word with the chaps who are check-ing over the garage and tell them exactly what to look out for. How's that?'

I shook my head, too dispirited to answer, for during this soothing little monologue I had been reviewing the events in the garage, in particular the scene where Walter had risen so manfully to the occasion and strode away to telephone Martin Graham, and it had dawned on me how foolishly I had under-rated him.

'You won't find it,' I said, after a long and most un-preg-nant pause. 'No, I'm not dotty. There really was a note of sorts, but I think I know now what's become of it, and also the gist of what it said.'

'Indeed? But I understood you to say you hadn't touched it?'

'No, but I've seen one like it before.'

'When was that?'

'About ten days ago, at Eglinton Hall. Someone threw a brick through the window and it had a note tied round it, in capital letters and red ink. It was some kind of warning or threat and it was signed by an outfit calling itself the Clean Up Britain Crusade, if that means anything to you?'

The atmosphere had lightened again. His manner was still guarded, but he was no longer contemplating me with the pitying disapproval which had been so painfully in evidence before.

'I've come across the name somewhere or other,' he admitted warily. 'And do you know what became of the first message?'

'As far as I know it was destroyed.'

'And we were not informed?'

'Well, no. The brick didn't cause much damage, you see, apart from a broken window, and as a family they're rather shy of publicity. I don't think they took it too seriously either; just put it down to a spiteful prank.'

'But you read the message? Can you recall what it said?'

'If you'll lend me your pen, I might. I can always see things better when I look at them,' I explained, a remark which oddly enough was one of the few to leave his eyebrows stationary. He obediently handed over a ballpoint and a sheet of paper, and after one or two false attempts I gave him the final version.

'I'll keep this,' he said, inserting it among his papers. 'Too bad the original was destroyed, but perhaps we'll have more luck with the one in the car. What do you think became of it?'

'It's all too obvious, I'm afraid. Walter must have removed it.'

'The student chap? I've got his statement here some-where—yes, here we are—Walter Greig, aged twenty-two . . . umm umm . . . doesn't make any reference to the subject, but conceivably we didn't ask him. Leaving aside motive, would he have had an opportunity to remove it?'

'The best. He was alone in the garage for all of five minutes while I rang you up. I thought he'd fainted, but he could have been shamming, or he could have come round and then caught sight of the golf club, which as you know was hanging half out of the car. He had plenty of time to remove the paper, but you won't find any prints because he had gloves with him.'

'So your theory is that he pocketed the note and then destroyed it? How? By flushing it down the lavatory?'

'Oh, nothing so crude. Thanks to my splendid co-operation, there was a far better way. I more or less sent him into the house to try and locate Mr Graham. All he had to do was walk through the main building and out by the back door and he'd be within five yards of the kiln. He could easily have shoved the paper inside because the doors open outwards, like a wardrobe, so there's no danger, even when it's going at full blast. If that's what he did, there'll be nothing left of it now.'

'Providing the kiln is in operation, but that's something we can very easily find out.'

The inspector laid a special emphasis on the last words, and again his eyebrows shot up to his hair line, but this time he was looking over my head, and the sergeant who had been sitting behind me got up and left the room.

'I bet you'll find it is,' I said when he had gone. 'They're getting a batch of stuff finished off for an exhibition. Firing is the final process, after the painting and glazing has been done, so it's bound to be running more or less continuously at present.'

'Well, we'll have another chat with the young man, but meantime do you know of any connection between him and these Clean Up people?'

'No direct connection, to be fair,' I admitted, 'but I've been thinking it over and oddly enough he is the common factor. I don't necessarily mean he was responsible but he was present on both occasions and each time he managed to create a certain amount of confusion.'

I described the events which had followed the brick throwing, omitting the theory which Kit had put forward concerning Walter's personal motive for beating him up because I no longer knew whether I believed this or not.

'He did not attempt to destroy the first message, however?' the Inspector asked.

'He didn't get the chance. Several other people were on it like hawks, but he may well have decided to be first in pursuit of the attacker, not to catch him, you understand, but to ensure that he got away.'

'Yes, I follow you, and that would seem to indicate that he had no part in Mrs Graham's murder.'

'Oh, really? Why does it do that?'

'Come, now! Why go to all the trouble of attaching a note to the weapon, simply to remove it again at the first opportunity, not even knowing whether anyone had seen it, or recognised it for what it was?'

'I hadn't thought of that,' I confessed. 'But it doesn't entirely let him out. Supposing the note was intended to scare one particular person, knowing that he or she, having seen it and been duly scared, could be depended upon to destroy it?'

'By he or she, you mean the lady's husband, I take it?'

'He's the most obvious one, don't you think? I mean, you do realise that my turning up when I did was pure fluke? I wasn't expected and if it hadn't been for the puncture, not a soul would have gone into the garage until Mr Graham returned. Walter keeps his bike outside. What's happened about the bike, incidentally? He seemed to be under the impression it had been stolen. Has it turned up yet?'

'Not as far as I know, but I've had rather more pressing matters to deal with, as you can appreciate, the most urgent being the whereabouts of Mr Graham. I don't suppose you can throw any light on that?'

'I only know what Walter told me; that he was spending the morning at the museum. Mrs Graham was to have dropped him off there and collected him after her golf lesson. But I expect you know all that?'

'Yes, and the first part went according to plan. He arrived at the museum just after ten and remained there until it closed. No one remembers seeing Mrs Graham but that doesn't mean much. It's a no parking area, so she wouldn't have been able to stop there for more than a minute or two.'

'But she did get to the golf course?'

'Yes, she was seen there by several people, though not after twelve thirty which is when she would have left to meet her husband.'

'Perhaps Sir Magnus Benson-Jones could fill in a bit more? That is if you can get close enough to ask him.'

'You are well informed, aren't you?' the inspector asked, smiling down at his notes.

'It's no secret that he was giving her lessons.'

'No, and we've already contacted him as it happens. He's been quite co-operative, you'll be glad to hear . . .' He broke off, and from that moment lost interest in me because the sergeant had returned, very breathless and pleased with himself.

'Excuse me interrupting, sir.'

'Yes, Jessell, what is it?'

'Mr Graham, sir. He's been found.'

'About time. Where?'

The sergeant tilted an eye in my direction, but evidently my stock remained high, for he got the signal to carry on.

'At the Radcliffe. He was brought in half an hour ago. Concussion and minor injuries.'

'What the hell? . . . What happened?'

'Knocked down by a car, from the look of it. He was found lying by the roadside, about midway between here and Eglinton.'

'Who found him?'

'A Mrs Paley, sir. She told the hospital authorities she saw him lying by the road and stopped her car. She was on her way to Oxford, so she took him aboard and dropped him off at the Radcliffe. Daft thing to do, of course, but she says he was conscious at the time and in some distress. Bleeding too, apparently. There wasn't a house within sight where she could telephone for the ambulance and she didn't care to leave him there. Apparently he passed out during the drive and he was still unconscious when she brought him in.'

The inspector stood up. 'Right. We'll get down there now and have a chat with him as soon as he wakes up. That's all for now thank you, Mrs Price, but I expect we'll be in touch with you shortly. Now, Jessell . . .'

Sergeant Jessell had left the door wide open on entering the room, so I followed his example when I left it, and heard him say:

'You mean to interview Graham yourself, sir?'

To which the inspector replied cheerfully: 'Oh yes, I think so. The sooner we get him talking the more likely we are to find out just how accidental an accident can be.'

CHAPTER THIRTEEN

'BY THE way, you had a caller,' Toby announced, when I had finished pouring out my tale into his intermittently attentive ear.

'Did I? Who was that?'

'The one you always say can't act for toffee.'

'Did I really say that? I suppose I must have, since I haven't a doubt who you mean. What was he doing down here?'

'Looking for you, presumably.'

'But how did he know where to find me?'

'He telephoned your London number and they gave him this one. He put two and two together and came in magnificent person.'

'To save the price of another telephone call?'

'I have an idea he was coming anyway. He mentioned that he was obligated to visiting the area. I can't remember why. I suppose I'd stopped listening. In any case, he threatens to return.'

'When?'

'About half past six, when we shall feel obligated to offer him a drink, no doubt.'

'I wonder what he wants? Not more yap yap about Henry's defence, I hope. Not that it matters now. They won't be able to hold Henry after this, will they?'

'Why not?'

'I should have thought it was obvious. The two murders must be connected. Henry couldn't have committed the second one, so it follows—what's the time, by the way?'

'Nearly six.'

'Bother! I wanted to ring Gerald and tell him to go into action, but he'll have left his office by now.'

'What's the hurry if it's as open and shut as you make out?'

'Well, no harm in giving him a nudge. I think I'll try his flat. Then he can get busy first thing in the morning.'

'Well, don't talk for hours,' Toby warned me. 'Your friend will be here soon and I have no intention of spending a single minute alone with him.'

'Don't worry, it's as good as done.'

*

'Oh no, it's not,' Gerald said. 'Sorry old scout, but you've got the wrong end of the stick.'

'But why, Gerald? There can't be two murderers operating in an area of this size.'

'On the contrary, old sport. You'd be surprised how infectious it can be.'

'You really mean they won't let Henry go now?'

'Not on your say-so, or mine either. There's a devil of a lot to be done before we reach that stage. And even then it's dicey. They think they've got all the evidence they need and, believe me, they won't let go that easily.'

'Well, damn it all, Gerald, you see what this means? We've not only still got the first murder hanging round our necks, we now have to solve the second one as well and tie them both up in one gift wrapped parcel.'

'Sooner you than me, old girl. And do make sure there isn't a third.'

'Oh, you bet. Listen, I've got to go now, Gerald. Someone's arrived. It's a bore, but he may put me on the track of something.'

I heard a faint groan from the other end before I rang off.

Kit was dead sober, but about as relaxed as a jumping bean. He brought me the news that Babs had been found dead in her own garage.

'I know. You're speaking to the one who found her.'

Whereupon he practically fainted away.

'I didn't know,' he said, when the heartbeats had reverted to normal. 'Toby never said a word.'

'He's only just heard. I've been assisting the police with their enquiries.'

'For Christ's sake, Tessa, it's not a joke. Don't you realise how ghastly it all is?'

'Better than you do, I daresay; and, incidentally, how did you get the news so fast?'

'I was lunching at the Hall and the police turned up. They wanted Magnus, but he'd gone to London. Actually, I think he's flying to Munich tonight, or one of those places. Anyway Julie played it a bit cagey so they told her what it was all about. Then naturally she gave them his office number.'

'You stagger me! She's not usually so co-operative with the law.'

'I'd just remind you that it was Julie who stopped Sarah being moved out of the tent.'

'I know, but she had two witnesses on that occasion. Anyway what happened next?'

'They asked if they could expedite things by ringing Magnus from the house. Julie took them out to the phone in the hall, where they more or less politely told her to get lost, so she didn't hear what they said. Apparently they got what they needed though, because they said they probably wouldn't have to bother her again.'

'So what's the panic?'

'No panic. Did I say there was?'

'Well, you tried to ring me in London, I understand?'

'Oh, that! Well, we felt we ought to contact you. Julie and I both agreed it would be better than your hearing about it on a news bulletin.'

Naturally, I didn't swallow this, such tender solicitude for my fragile nerves being somewhat out of character, but I concluded it was the best excuse he could drum up at short notice and I was not yet ready to disillusion him.

'And to be absolutely frank with you,' he went on, in an absolutely frank way, 'it had hit us both that you could have been right about Henry, after all. It's darn lucky for him, of course, the way things have turned out, but one has to accept that there's a homicidal maniac on the loose, and the police have fallen flat on their faces. We can all see that now, but one has to hand it to you for guessing it all along.'

'That's mighty handsome of you, Kit.'

'No, it's Julie should take the credit,' he admitted, battling gamely on with the rueful little boy act. 'It was almost the first thing she thought of, after the police had left. She really grabbed the chance to contact you right away and offer to help with expediting Henry's release.'

'How very magnanimous of her!'

'Okay, so you don't like her, but she's really a great human being, let me tell you. She may not have Sarah's charisma, but she's a very warm person. Her first thought, once she was over the shock, was to tell you that she . . . well, Magnus, really . . . had been totally wrong about Henry. You could hardly say fairer than that, could you?'

'No, and you could hardly say more arrogant, either. What sauce to imagine that either she or her father could have prevented the police arresting the entire population if they'd had a mind to. And if you wonder why I'm not specially drawn to her, there's your answer. It's not so much the actual power which people of their sort wield, it's their delusions of power which make them so terribly tedious and unreal. However, I wouldn't expect you to agree; and why the quick turnabout? I thought you were the one who had no time for Julie?'

'Me? You have to be joking!'

'Well, I happen to know that she was cut to the quick when you sped off to the continent last week without even waving goodbye.'

Kit was so transparent sometimes that one could monitor the thoughts passing through his so-called brain as easily as though they were running across his forehead on a telex tape. When he had got the latest batch sorted out, he put on a matching face and said,

'This is going to sound big-headed, I know, but try to understand. I'm devoted to Julie, but only like she was my sister. You see, I was in love with Sarah. It's as simple as that.'

'And you had begun to feel that Julie did not love you quite as a brother?'

'Right. You probably saw what was happening way in advance of when I did. It always knocks me out to find that someone has a thing about me. When I finally got around to it, I realised I was getting involved up to my neck. I didn't want to hurt her. Christ, she's had enough knocks in her life! I thought maybe if I were just to fade out for a bit it would give her time to cool off. She would realise she was only getting to feel that way because she was missing Sarah and desperately needed someone to put in her place. Given time to rationalise her emotions, she'd see they weren't nearly so deep as she'd imagined.'

'Well, bully for you! If only we could all solve our problems so easily!'

'What the hell does that mean?'

'I refer to the magic properties of your anti-love potion. The cooling off process seems to have been more rapid than even you could have anticipated. Just think of it!

You discover what the rest of us have known all along, but you're not in the market, so you go to Rome and Paris for precisely five days. At the end of that time, absence has made the heart so much less fond that you can come down and have lunch with her today, just like brother and sister again.'

'You've got it all wrong as it happens, Tessa, but I don't have to justify myself to you, do I?'

'No, so let's not discuss it; but I didn't seek you out, remember?'

'I had to come down today,' he said sulkily. 'There wasn't any option. If you must know, Julie wanted to see me about Sarah's will. There was a letter from her at the flat when I flew in from Paris, asking me to go down there and discuss it. I could hardly refuse.'

'I suppose not. Has she left you a packet?'

'Christ, no, I shouldn't think so for a minute. Probably just some personal mementoes or something.'

'Don't you know? You mean you went all that way purposely to discuss it and then you didn't discuss it at all?'

'There wasn't time . . . well, you know . . . we'd just got around to talking about it in general terms when the fuzz came—anyway what the hell does it matter?'

'Well if I were you, Kit, I'd mug up a bit on this part and get your facts straight. It could be important.'

'How come?'

'Don't you see that you only have to produce this letter of Julie's and give an account of what passed between you this morning and you both have a reasonably tidy little alibi for Mrs Graham's murder. Hadn't that occurred to you?'

I cannot tell whether the answer he finally produced was the same as he would have given spontaneously for at this point there was an interruption, lasting for several minutes, which altered the tenor of our subsequent conversation. Toby put his head round the door and announced that I was wanted on the telephone, withdrawing it again before I could ask who by.

When I returned, Kit, having refilled his glass, was toasting his reflection in the mirror over the fireplace, and I said,

'You'll have to drink that down sharpish. I've got to go out.'

'Where to? Want me to drop you off?'

'No, thanks. It's out of your way, if you're going to London. I'm Dedley bound.'

'What do you want to go there for?'

He was still gazing complacently into the mirror, twitching his tie about, and I could not resist bursting the narcissistic bubble.

'I don't want to, it's an order. Chief Detective Inspector Payne has requested my presence.'

Watching his reflection, I saw his jaw drop as he put out both hands and clutched the chimney piece to steady himself. Then rallying again, he picked up his glass, saying with a great show of indifference,

'What a bore! What do they want now? I thought they'd squeezed you dry?'

'So did I but something fresh has come up, something I might have seen before the murder was committed, apparently. He wouldn't go into details. I told him I'd be there in half an hour so I can't hang about much longer.'

Kit ignored this.

'They must be out of their minds! How could you have anything meaningful to tell them about what happened before the murder?'

'I've told you, I don't know. And I'll probably have enough trouble answering the inspector's questions, without bothering with yours. So would you kindly get a move on?'

'Oh, stop fussing. Basically, they have no right to send out orders like this. You ought to stand up to them and refuse to go. Personally, I'd see them in hell first.'

'I'm afraid I can't agree. If I do possess some vital evidence, it makes me rather vulnerable, wouldn't you say?

For my own protection, I'd be a mug not to tell them about it at the soonest possible moment.'

I had been fidgeting by the door as I spoke, and now grasped the knob in the manner of one who would brook no further delay, but in fact I was not in half such a hurry as I pretended, considering that it would be time well spent if I could finally goad Kit into betraying what was really on his mind, and there were signs that this was at last about to occur. He threw his cigarette into the fire and said quietly, hardly moving his lips,

'Let's get this straight, shall we, Tessa? Did you or did you not see anything?'

'Like what?' I asked, moving back a few steps away from the door and resting my arms along the back of an armchair. 'Or should I say, like whom?'

'Oh, hell! That means you did. I've had this feeling all along. But why not be frank about it? You surely can't suspect her of being implicated?'

'It's not my job to suspect anyone of anything. I assume we're taking about Julie?'

'You know darn well we are.'

'Who wasn't at home when you answered her summons this morning? Which is the true reason why you never got around to discussing Sarah's will? Did she tell you she'd been at Missendale?'

'Yes, that is . . . no . . . no, she didn't.'

'But you guessed? Is that it?'

'She wasn't there when I arrived, see? Although I was a bit late, as it happened. I waited about ten minutes and then she came in. She told me the butler had made a mistake saying she was out. She'd been in her room all the time.'

'And you believed her, naturally?'

'Sure. Why not? She moves around pretty quietly and it was feasible the butler really had got it wrong. It wasn't until the police came and she got in such a goddam flap that I began to have doubts. And when they'd gone she said . . . she asked me, if it ever came up, to swear we'd been together the whole time. But if you saw her at Missendale . . . ?'

'Well I didn't, if that's any comfort to you. Not that it will do her much good, will it?'

'Why not? You surely wouldn't repeat what I've told you?'

'No, but there's still the butler.'

'Oh, him!'

'Yes, him. If he's asked, he's bound to say she was out when you arrived.'

'So what? He could have been mistaken and anyway it's only his word against hers and mine. Also I don't see that bunch doing anything to wreck their jobs. It's not just Fernando and his wife, you know, the whole family works in the house. They have everything to lose.'

'You've strayed into Benson-Jones dreamland by the sound of it. However, if you want to believe that money conquers all, don't let me stop you. Are you ready to leave now?'

'No, you won't stop me,' he agreed, as we walked out to the Common where our cars were standing. 'And if it comes to it, I wouldn't have any objections to saying that I went up to her room and found her writing to Aunt Maud, or whatever. You know why?'

'Yes, I know why. Because you believe that whatever Julie was doing, whether at Missendale or not, she is innocent of any crime, past, present or future. And the reason why you believe that is because it suits you to.'

'Oh, drop dead!' he said, getting into the Bentley and slamming the door. He then rolled the window down to deliver the parting shot.

'You can think what you bloody please. It's nothing to me.'

I did not quite believe him. The evidence showed that he cared a good deal what I thought, and had bared his soul in order to find out what it was. Nevertheless, one question remained unanswered. There was no telling whether his concern for Julie was genuine, or whether indeed he had made up the whole story while I was out of the room, conceivably with the aim of blurring any memory I might retain of a white Bentley parked outside the *Eglinton Arms* when I slowed down to make the sharp left turn for Missendale.

CHAPTER FOURTEEN

1

'AND what have you been up to now?' Robin asked me. 'You don't have to answer unless you wish to,' he added politely. 'I am not here officially.'

'Oh, good! Where are you officially?'

'Still writing up my report. It didn't take as long as I'd expected so I'm giving myself a few hours off.'

'And spending them at the Dedley police station?'

'I am not sure that my unofficial status gives you the right to ask all the questions, but the answer to the last one is that I got wind of some funny goings on at Missendale Potteries and I deemed it advisable to come down and do some checking up.'

'Well, I'm delighted to see you, and I only wish you would deem that kind of thing more often. However, I imagine you're not the sole reason for my being invited to the party?

Wasn't there something you wanted to ask me?' I said, addressing the last question to Inspector Payne, who had been a patient audience throughout the preceding dialogue, although giving his eyebrows a good deal of exercise. 'No trace of that message from the Cleaners, I suppose?'

'Not so far, Mrs Price, but we've found something else. The missing bike, no less.'

'Good for you! Where was it?'

'In the woods, just off the road, and not five hundred yards from the Potteries. We may have a little identification job for you later on, but meanwhile there's something we'd like you to point out to us, if you can spare half an hour?'

'Gladly. What can it be, I wonder?'

'The exact spot where you stopped your car this morning, when you realised your tyre was going down. I take it you can remember roughly?'

'Yes, it's the only straight section for several miles and I aimed for the halfway point, but I can't see how it's going to help you.'

'Shall we trot along there, then?' the inspector asked, ignoring this. 'The car's outside.'

He stood up and Robin and I followed him out of the room.

I felt a shade uneasy during the drive. It was ridiculous to suppose that the inspector had seen through my ruse, or that, even if he had, this solemn little procession to the scene of my crime would have appealed to one who led such a full and busy life. Nevertheless, the uncomfortable doubts persisted and I could not even keep my spirits up with innocent chatter to Robin because he sat in front with the uniformed driver and I shared the back seat with Inspector Payne, a disposition of personnel which also struck me as faintly sinister.

We rounded the last bend before the road straightened out and he tapped on the driver's shoulder as a signal to slow down, at the same time turning enquiringly to me.

'Somewhere along here?'

'Another fifty yards,' I agreed. 'I wanted to give myself the best chance of being seen from both directions and there was no urgency. I could pick my own spot,' I added, sounding defensive in spite of myself.

'Which, conversely, means that you had an excellent opportunity to observe the motor cyclist, both before and after he passed you?'

'Not before. I heard him, of course, but I was bending down and the car blocked my view. I did see him from behind because when he passed me at such a lunatic speed I was naturally curious to take a look at him.'

'Did you recognise him?'

'Sorry, no. He was wearing the usual gear and I only got a view of his back. His way of driving was a trifle reminiscent but I don't suppose that would count as evidence.'

'It's all too common, unfortunately. How about the bike? You didn't note the number, by any chance?'

'There wasn't time. I doubt if I'd have thought of it, even if there had been.'

'I see. And how fast do you estimate he was travelling?'

'I'd say sixty, at least; perhaps more. I wish you'd tell me what this is all about.'

'Yes, but just bear with me a little longer, Mrs Price. First, I'd like you to tell me exactly what occurred next.'

'Why nothing. I just got back in my car and drove on. I'd checked the tyre, you see, and I knew it wasn't bad enough to affect the steering very seriously, and I thought that by taking it slowly I might get to a garage before I was in real trouble. In fact, I didn't pass one, but I found myself at

Missendale and I stopped at the Grahams' to ask if I could borrow a pump.'

'Ah! So you were driving very slowly? Somewhere around twenty miles an hour, would that be?'

'Something like that. Why?'

'So that you'd have been particularly well placed to notice any pedestrian, either approaching or proceeding in the same direction as yourself?'

'Yes, I suppose so, although I don't remember one.'

'You're sure of that?'

On firmer ground now, I said, 'Yes, I am sure, but it doesn't prove there weren't any. I was concentrating on my own troubles and also it had occurred to me by then that I must be somewhere near the Grahams' place so I was looking out for that. I could have passed half a dozen pedestrians, I suppose, without consciously registering the fact.'

'Even if you had recognised one of them?'

'No, obviously that would have been different. I suppose you're thinking of Martin Graham? I am sure I would have noticed him and stopped. After all, it was his house I was making for.'

'And, purely as a formality, did you notice anyone lying by the road?'

'No, I didn't. Whereabout was he found?'

'According to this Mrs Paley who picked him up, it was about half a mile from here.'

'On which side.'

'The right, from your point of view. She was coming the other way.'

'Well, that accounts for it. It puts him on her nearside doesn't it? Whereas there could very easily have been a car between him and myself when I passed. I was going at such a crawl that I was overtaken by practically everything on the road.'

Robin had taken no part in the interrogation but, catching his eye from time to time, I had seen him watching me thoughtfully and felt relieved to have glided into the area of factual reporting. As though recognising this, he now focused attention on Inspector Payne.

'Well, it was worth a try, Arnold, but it seems your prize witness hasn't come up with anything you didn't already know.'

'Oh, I wouldn't say that,' he answered placidly. 'None of it contradicts certain assumptions we'd already made, which is a step in the right direction, and Mrs Price may be able to add something when she's seen the bike.'

'Where exactly was it dumped?' I asked, when we were back in the car.

'A hundred yards or so from where Mr Graham was allegedly knocked down.'

'A mere step from the Potteries, in fact?'

'Correct. So even if young Walter was to blame, he could still have walked the rest of the way home and arrived there ahead of you. On the other hand he insists that his bike must have been stolen between ten o'clock this morning, when the Grahams went out, and around two when you arrived. He seems positive that if it had gone before they left they'd have noticed and told him about it.'

'And what's Mr Graham's version of the accident?'

'He claims not to know what hit him, far less who. A complete mental black out, as you might say. Still, that's common enough at this stage. When the shock wears off the memory may return.'

'And the bike? Was there anything to show that it had been involved in a collision?'

'You'd have made a good policeman, Mrs Price.'

This was not exactly answering the question, but I could hardly complain about that because I was equally unhelpful when it came to dictating my own statement. I was not required to advance any theories as to the ownership of the motor cycle, since it had already been traced to Walter through the registration number, but I could produce no information at all about the one which had passed me on the road, far less identify its driver.

2

'Still on the subject of motor vehicles,' Robin said, as we drove back to Roakes, 'did you ever get this one fixed? Think carefully before answering.'

I did so, taking so long about it that he may have thought I had missed the point, for he went on:

'Arnold tells me that he got one of his boys to pump up the tyre for you, but did you ever have time to take it to a garage to be repaired? It doesn't do to neglect these things.'

'Okay, okay,' I said crossly. 'No need to labour it. I guessed I hadn't fooled you but what you should remember is that the outcome would have been exactly the same, whether it had been a false puncture or a genuine one.'

'How so?'

'Simply that my letting out the air on purpose didn't change anything. If Nature, or whoever is in charge of these matters, had done it for me, I'd still have played safe and stopped where I did. I'd still have driven on at a snail's pace and I'd still have made straight for the Potteries. So what's the odds?'

'Just this, my poor girl. If you'd never contrived the business at all you wouldn't have been parked at that particular point when the accident occurred. In other words, you might have seen it happen.'

'Well, yes, I hadn't thought of that.'

'Don't think I'm complaining. For once your deviousness seems to have kept you out of trouble instead of pitching you headlong into it. I just thought it was worth pointing out.'

'On the other hand there might not have been an accident if there'd been a witness.'

'Oh, so you believe that was contrived too?'

'Martin could have fixed it, you know, having murdered his wife and needing to fix himself up with an alibi. At least I gathered the inspector's inscrutable mind was working along those lines.'

'Not altogether.'

'No? What's changed it?'

'He's seen Graham now, and heard the doctor's report. The injuries are not serious, but neither are they of the type to have been self-inflicted. Furthermore there are stains and tears on his clothes which are consistent with his being in some kind of collision. I don't doubt that the analysts will find matching evidence on the bike.'

'All the same, if he'd stolen it, he might still have faked all that and then flopped down by the road, waiting to be rescued.'

'Having first disposed not only of the bike, but also of the leather jacket and the helmet and goggles?'

'Yes, that does make it awkward, I admit. But what does he say about it himself?'

'Well, he's lucid enough, up to a point. As I told you, his injuries are quite superficial. In fact, they're sending him home in the morning. Arnold rather pressed for it. I think he's curious to see what he gets up to.'

'Lucid up to what point?'

'To the period immediately before the accident; but, as you heard, most people get a blessed amnesia of that kind. All they know is that one minute they were walking along, whistling a merry tune and the next thing is they're waking up in hospital.'

'It's particularly convenient in Martin's case, wouldn't you say?'

'Maybe, but it could also be true.'

'Does he remember why he was on the road at all?'

'Yes, all that part is perfectly clear and has been confirmed by unbiased witnesses. His wife dropped him off at the museum and then went on to play golf. The arrangement was that she would call for him around twelve thirty and drive him home to lunch.'

'But she didn't?'

'No. He says she telephoned just before she was due to say she'd been held up. The curator's secretary confirms that a call did come through for him at about that time, and he took it in her office. Unfortunately she's rather a prim lady and she left him to hold his conversation in private. Also she didn't ask the caller's name, which is fairly annoying of her, but she's pretty certain it was a woman.'

'And did Babs explain why she had been held up?'

'I'm not sure about that but he says that, as the museum is closed between one and three, she suggested he should go along to the pub for a snack and a drink and she'd join him there as soon as she could.'

'Which pub? Not the *Eglinton Arms* by any chance?'

'Yes, I do believe that was the name. Why? Is it important?'

'Could be, but go on. Did he do that?'

'Yes, he walked in at about twenty past one. The place was packed but the landlord knows him and remembers it well.'

'How did he get there? On foot?'

'Presumably. Why?'

'Well, it must be at least a mile from the museum. Wasn't it rather a curious rendezvous in the circumstances?'

'Not necessarily. There was nothing he could do there, once the staff had departed for lunch, so he had time to kill. And I must tell you that even if he had borrowed or pinched a car, he wouldn't have had time to drive to the Potteries, murder his wife and get back to the pub by twenty past one. And he did get there. The landlord is certain of it.'

'Ah!'

'Yes, I know. When people have a particular recollection of the time it often means there's something phoney about it; but there are exceptions and this appears to be one of them. As you might expect, it was the peak period of the day, when all the regulars come and go at the same time, every Monday to Friday, and the publican could give you a reasonable estimate of the time simply by looking round at the faces in the bar. There was the usual crush this morning and Graham elected to take his beer and sandwiches to a table outside. He paid for the lot and carried them out himself, and that was the last they saw of him.'

'Did his wife turn up?'

'No one seems to know. Just after two o'clock the bar-maid went out to tidy up. No one was there, just an empty plate and glass on one of the tables, which was exactly as it should have been; but we now take up the tale as told by Graham himself.'

'Good! I've been looking forward to that.'

'He maintains that his wife never came. He waited for over half an hour and then got bored and decided to start walking.'

'Without leaving a message for her?'

'Apparently he expected to meet her on the road. The golf course is roughly in the Missendale direction.'

'And then what?'

'Very little. He remembers passing a cottage called 'Oakdene' because the owners have a collie which barks its head off every time someone approaches. He admits to being nervous of dogs and when he heard this one going into its usual hysteria he crossed over and gave it a wide berth. There's a slight discrepancy there, incidentally.'

'Hooray! What is it?'

'Well, from that point on his mind is a complete blank, and in fact he was found not far away, but on the right of the road, that's to say the same side as Oakdene.'

'You think he may have invented the bit about the dog, in order to lend colour to his story?'

'Yes, or he could have been in the act of crossing back when he was knocked down. It's almost instinctive with some people to face the oncoming traffic when they're walking on country roads. It's odd though, because as you know so well he would already have passed along the straight section, where it would have been safer and more natural to have crossed over. It's the only part of his story which raises faint doubts.'

'Then you and Arnold are more easily satisfied than I am. I can find doubts which, placed end to end, would stretch from here to life imprisonment. I don't mean that it couldn't all have happened as he describes it; but take that telephone call to the museum, for a start. Supposing Babs had just said that she couldn't collect him and left it at that? It's not improbable because if Magnus had invited her to play another round she'd have jumped at it. She wouldn't have had the slightest compunction in ditching Martin, I'm willing to bet.'

'No takers. I'm willing to bet on it too.'

'All right, so instead of arranging to meet him at the pub, he's to make his own way home and she'll be back as soon as she can. He agrees to this and sets up the alibi with the beer and sandwiches. But instead of sitting down to them he simply canters off home across the fields. Not much risk of anyone noticing him go, since they're so busy at that time, and he could have been home in twenty minutes.'

'To take up his position in the garage, awaiting his wife's return? Is that the idea?'

'Yes, and having whacked her over the head and attached the note to the golf club to give a false lead, he wheels Walter's bike out on to the road. All that remains is to drive it a few hundred yards, ditch it in the woods, collapse on the roadside and go into his concussion act. He could easily have inflicted a few cuts and bruises to make it look authentic.'

'Well, that's a nice, neat theory in a way,' Robin said, 'but there's just one snag.'

'What's that?'

'It gives us the premise of two somewhat eccentric drivers on two separate bikes operating within minutes of each other on the same stretch of country lane. The one who passed you was not only wearing all the proper gear, he was also heading towards the Potteries and not away from them.'

'I'm prepared to write that off as coincidence. After all, the roads are chock-a-block with them, and Walter's not the only tearaway.'

'Which reminds me: did you get the impression that he was genuinely surprised to find his bike was missing, or could it have been an act?'

'It's hard to say. I'd already seen Babs by then, and I was fairly certain she was dead. It's the kind of thing which doesn't leave much room for other kinds of speculation. And

I can't quite make Walter out. Most of the time he appears to be slightly moronic, but occasionally one glimpses a crafty side as well. On the other hand, Robin, what possible motive could he have had for murdering either of these two women?'

'Unless there's some connection with the Clean Up People?'

'That's possible, I suppose, with his background. And Sarah could well have been on the list of people to be eliminated. I suppose it could also have been his reason for beating up Kit. I could never swallow the idea of his doing it for love of Sarah, but if his object was to ensure that Kit was so groggy that he wouldn't realise or remember that Walter was covering the attacker's retreat, instead of going after him, then there would have been method in his madness. But where does Babs fit in with that theory?'

'Perhaps she'd rumbled him and he had to kill her out of self-protection? If there had been any hanky panky over the students' overalls, to name but one possibility, Babs would have been the most likely person to know about it.'

'You're quite right, Robin, it all hangs together splendidly. Now, the only thing is, how are we going to pin it on him?'

'Ah well, as to that, I'm afraid you'll have to count me out,' he said, pretending to take the question very seriously. 'I have one or two problems of my own on hand at present. Besides, it's rather your forte, isn't it? I'm sure we can safely leave the whole thing to you and Arnold.'

2

'I've been thinking over the case against Walter,' I announced the following morning. 'And I'm sorry to say that I've hit a gigantic snag.'

'Oh, tough luck!' Robin said absently. He was packing his case to go back to London, and not, I suspect, giving his entire mind to what I was saying.

'Yes, the difficulty lies in reconciling his being a member of the Clean Up Brigade and also a student at Missendale. Surely there would have been something in his background to connect him with racialism and so on? Martin Graham told me that it was largely through Magnus's sponsorship that Walter got a place here, and Magnus, as you know, is very hot on details.'

'Yes, it's a point, but I expect you'll find a way round it. He may not be the real Walter, you know; just someone impersonating him. Or perhaps he had a good record when he came here and only got converted to the Cleaners afterwards?'

'Well, I suppose that can happen. Perhaps Arnold ought to do a little checking on this mysterious friend in Oxford? It might be a pseudonym for the gang. But speaking of Magnus reminds me of something else I wanted to ask you: wasn't he able to throw any light on Babs' movements?'

'Oh yes, plenty, but none of it does a thing for yesterday's case against Graham or today's case against Walter.'

'Oh, how dull! What did he say?'

'That he was entirely to blame for the fact that she cancelled the arrangement with her husband.'

'Not that he had to twist her arm, presumably?'

'No, and he wasn't even aware that she'd made one. What happened was that on the way to meet her for the golf lesson he stopped off at the local garage because his self-starter was playing up and he wanted to get it fixed before he drove to London in the afternoon. They told him it might take some time, so he used one of their hire cars, plus driver, to take him on to the club. The same man was to collect him again at twelve thirty and drive him back to the garage.'

'Doesn't he have a chauffeur to take care of these things for him?'

'Yes, that did come up, but it seems that the chauffeur is employed by the company and Magnus makes a point of only using him for company business. Apparently he's very meticulous in these matters.'

'And also it probably suits his youthful, jaunty image to dash around the countryside behind the wheel of his sports car. Go on, though.'

'Well, he related all this to Babs during her lesson and, for some reason which he either doesn't understand or is too modest to acknowledge, she insisted on driving him to the garage in her car. However, he claims that he had no idea that this would mean breaking an appointment with her husband.'

'Hang on! What about her telephone call?'

'There is no proof that she actually made one, but Magnus certainly did.'

'Oh?'

'To cancel the arrangement with the garage. He went away to do this and she told him she was going to powder her nose. They met up again ten minutes later in the bar. She said nothing about having made a call herself, but in fact the time coincides with the one which came through to the museum, and also there's a coin box in the ladies' changing room.'

'Which garage was it?'

'The one at Eglinton. The story was checked, naturally, and they confirm that when he rang up to ask if his car was ready he was told it was and that he could collect it whenever he liked. In fact he did so between one and one-fifteen.'

'And Babs was with him?'

'Yes, although they could easily have missed that, seeing that it was the lunch hour and there weren't many of them around. However, it just so happened that the man on the petrol pumps did see him arrive and get into his car, and did see Babs drive away in hers. So, in fact, Tessa, although your reconstruction may be basically right, I think you've made it unnecessarily complicated. She would have been quite near the pub by then, so what was to prevent her going on there, as arranged? Martin could then have driven home with her and carried out the rest of the programme exactly as you described it.'

'But in that case, wouldn't someone have seen her arrive at the *Eglinton Arms*?'

'Conceivably someone will turn up who did, which would certainly blow Graham's story into tiny fragments, but I doubt very much if he'd have told it unless he'd felt on safe ground. The car park was probably full at the time, so she may well have driven on and stopped round the corner. If so, Graham would have seen this happen and gone out to join her. She need never have left the car at all.'

'So, one way and another, things are beginning to look rather black for poor old Martin?'

'Oh, he's poor old Martin now, is he? Well, don't worry, there's a long way to go before he's in real trouble, particularly if the two murders are connected.'

'And you agree with me that they must be?'

'Yes,' he replied. 'On the whole, I do.'

'And also that there's a link of some kind with the Cleaners?'

'Yes, to that too. I have a feeling that the Cleaners fit into the pattern somewhere. Curiously enough, I've been on the track of something very similar myself, during the past week or two. There's a kind of international Ku Klux Klan in operation, with link-ups all over the world. Ostensibly it's a crusade against communism, but there are some rather more disagreeable features as well. You'd be surprised to hear of the countries where they've managed to get a foothold; including our own, I regret to say. But that's a long story, and I really haven't time to go into it now, Tessa. In fact if I don't get a move on I shall be in trouble.'

I recognised the tone and knew it would be useless to try and coerce him into further disclosures. It was a nuisance because his last remarks had suddenly opened up a whole new range of possibilities, and I was longing to follow them up. Unfortunately I have never managed to overcome a rather childish resentment at being kept in the dark, and must confess to a certain ambiguity when Robin said,

'Well, goodbye, love. I may have to go abroad again tomorrow, but only for a couple of days. What are your plans?'

'Perhaps I'll stay on here for a bit, in that case,' I replied. 'I've had a rather pressing invitation.'

CHAPTER FIFTEEN

1

NOR did I take Toby into my confidence. On the erroneous assumption that the fewer people who knew about my movements the better, I simply allowed him to believe that I was going back to London.

Julie was ecstatic over the news and I had the alarming impression that she counted on my staying for at least a week. This was not my intention, for although two of the five items on my agenda could best be accomplished as an inmate of Eglinton Hall, I hoped to conclude them in a matter of hours and had no desire to prolong my visit unnecessarily.

However, there were other matters to be dealt with before this and the memory of a stray remark of Robin's set the wheels in motion for the first. Acting on his advice, I took the car to the Eglinton Garage and explained that one of the tyres had a slow puncture. There was a slight hold up while I puzzled out which one it was, but as soon as that was sorted out the mechanic obligingly changed the wheel for me and while he was doing so I asked him a question or two about the Grahams' car. The answers came out much as I had anticipated and the exhilaration of discovering I was on the right track provided a much needed boost for the next hurdle.

I had been distinctly apprehensive about approaching Dr Simmons, for he had a most discouraging manner, but I had asked for an appointment as a private patient so at least he was getting paid for my importunity and maybe the fact that two people in the neighbourhood had been brutally murdered did something to induce a more lenient response than I would otherwise have got.

In fact he quite naturally refused to give me any information in open terms, explaining that it would be unethical to do so, but when I had rephrased the questions in a form which required merely a nod or shake of the head, he grudgingly fell into line, and once again the answers came out precisely as I had expected.

It was four o'clock when I arrived at the Hall, and Julie welcomed me in a state of repressed excitement which I could not attribute solely to her pleasure in seeing me, although she went on a good deal about that too.

She took me up to the bedroom which had been allotted to me before, and I became rather disenchanted with millionaireville when I discovered that the waste paper basket had not been emptied since my previous visit, nor the sheets changed on the four poster. However, some allowance had to be made for a household which had been the scene of a major tragedy and furthermore Julie explained that she had allowed the staff the weekend off, since it was the first free time they had had since Sarah's death, but had foolishly forgotten to give instructions about my room before they left.

'I'm afraid I'm rather an amateurish housekeeper,' she told me, endeavouring to look contrite about it, but unable to conceal the inner complacency. 'Sarah was so marvellously efficient that one never had to give it a thought. But I expect I'll get the hang of it soon, and these are your own sheets, so perhaps you won't mind using them again.'

'Not a bit. I'm quite used to it.'

'And there'll be armies of daily women coming up from the village tomorrow, so we don't have to worry about cleaning or anything. Or meals, either. Cooking is one of my few talents.'

'Oh, really? Where did you learn that?'

'I did some courses at the Women's Institute. I don't often get the chance to put my skills into practice, but I'm preparing a very special supper for us this evening, so I do hope you're going to enjoy it.'

She burbled on in this strain for a while, then left me to unpack while she went downstairs to get started with the chopping and marinating.

It provided an unforeseen opportunity for proceeding with the next part of the programme, but as this involved an expedition to one of the other bedrooms, I decided to pass it up. This was partly funk, admittedly, but strategy was involved as well. For one thing, it was a particularly grey afternoon and a good light was essential for my purpose. Moreover, Julie's bubbling mood was hardly conducive to a protracted solitary spell in the kitchen, and I fully expected her to come hobbling upstairs again at any moment on the pretext of ascertaining whether I liked garlic in the stew. My chances of success might well suffer a setback if she were to discover me roaming round the family's private apartments.

The salmon mousse and stuffed veal were well up to Women's Institute standards, and the wine in excess of them. Julie became quite maudlin, telling me about fourteen times how much she enjoyed my company. It was a sad reflection on the dreariness of her life that dinner in the kitchen with a female she had known for barely a fortnight should have constituted such a highlight, but I was not disposed to carp about that.

It proved almost too easy to draw her out on the subject of Sarah, and in fact she drooled on so repetitively about their unique relationship and single minded devotion that I began to regret having picked this as my jumping off point. To steer her on to more prosaic lines, I said:

'As you know, I only met her so briefly, but there was one thing which puzzled me a lot about Sarah.'

'Well yes, I expect there were several. She was a very complex character in some ways and except with me she had great areas of reserve.'

'I daresay most people have, but I'm speaking of a purely superficial trait which must have struck everyone when they first met her.'

'I can't imagine what that could be,' Julie said in a rather haughty tone.

'Perhaps you took everything about her so much for granted that you'd ceased to notice; or perhaps you understood that it was a cover-up of some kind and were able to discount it.'

'Oh, no, that's quite out of the question You must have misunderstood her completely if you believed her capable of deceit in any form. She was the most straightforward person in the world. In fact, if she had a fault it was in being a little too opinionated and outspoken. If she saw anything which needed putting right she couldn't rest until it was done, no matter who she offended.'

'Yes,' I agreed, 'that's exactly what I'd been led to expect, and yet, you know Julie, from an outsider's point of view, she was not like that at all. Superficially, at any rate, she was riddled with self doubt and practically incapable of making the most trivial decision without clamouring for reassurance from all sides. Maybe it was just a pose, but that doesn't seem to be quite in character either.'

Julie was staring at me, open mouthed and incredulous, but I could not tell whether the passage of time had already put even such mild criticism on the level of heresy, or whether she was genuinely bewildered. To help things along, I said,

'Well, that's how it appeared to me, at any rate, and what really interests me is whether she was always like that, or whether it was only a recent phase. This is not aimless curiosity, you know. I suspect she may have been in an abnormal state during the few days before her death, and I honestly believe that if we knew the cause it might help us to find out why she was murdered.'

That did it. In a typically clumsy gesture which nearly sent a plate flying, Julie brought her elbows up on to the table and covered her face with her hands, as though the mere sight of me was unbearable. Clearly, I had lost my advantage and, with shock tactics as the only weapon left, I said,

'And the same goes for Kit, incidentally. We're not great friends, but I've had ample opportunity to observe his behaviour, and I can tell you that he wasn't at all himself that weekend. For one thing, have you ever known him get so drunk as he did? Are you listening, Julie?'

She slightly shook her head, then nodded, and, unable to guess whether she had answered the questions in sequence, there was nothing for it but to plough on.

'I know he drinks a lot, but it doesn't normally get out of hand, and that's the only time I've seen him literally incapable. I think it's partly because he's vain about his looks and keeps himself in such marvellous physical trim that alcohol doesn't usually affect him very much. But it certainly did that evening. He was absolutely sodden and I keep wondering why.'

She still did not utter a word, though now jerking her head spasmodically, as though to shake off a persistent wasp, and I kept going:

'Because, you see, there wasn't any apparent reason for it. You could argue that everyone is liable to go overboard once in a while, but why then? There he was, reunited with Sarah, and four days' holiday ahead. So far as one could tell, there hadn't been a cross word between them, and everyone was being radiant to him. Even your father, who might conceivably have disapproved, told me that he was in favour of the marriage. So what had gone wrong?'

I dragged an answer out of her at last, but it was a pretty dusty one. She removed her hands from her face, but only to bracket them in a shield above her eyes, and she said in a listless voice:

'I don't know, Tessa. I really don't understand what you're driving at. I keep recalling that evening, when it seems to me now that we were all happy for the very last time. And you fitted in so well. Sarah had been nervous, but she took to you at once, and so did Magnus. Everything had been going so beautifully, and then it all started to fall apart. Looking back, I'd somehow associated that with the Grahams, but I don't know; maybe the rot set in even before they came. I'm sorry, Tessa, but I can't seem to concentrate properly. Perhaps I've had too much wine or something, but I feel I should go to bed now, if you'll excuse me.'

She stood up and stumbled over to the door, and I followed her out of the room and upstairs to the gallery. It was a boring and faintly ludicrous ascent, because the combined effects of lameness and alcohol required her to grip the banister and drag herself up like a small child, one step at a time and I felt it would be tactless to overtake her and proceed at a normal pace. However, we made it at last and the exercise had evidently cleared her head a little, for at the top she turned to me in a plucky imitation of Sarah's hostessy manner, saying,

'Sorry to be so frightfully dim. I'll be fine in the morning. Goodnight, Tessa. I do hope you sleep well.'

2

The hope was not realised. Possibly I had been over-lavish with the wine myself, but in the dragging solitude of the hours before dawn, when even the stirrings of queasiness herald the onset of a fatal disease, it struck me, among other depressing contingencies, that the salmon mousse might not have been quite up to the mark. I would have given ten years of my life to have had Robin on call to bring some common sense to bear on the situation, and for lack of it lay awake groaning in self pity for what seemed like several long nights strung together, before falling asleep with the daylight.

It was past ten o'clock when I woke, but not having expected to open my eyes on another day, the hour was immaterial. There was a breakfast tray on my bedside table, and a note from Julie propped against the coffee pot, which read as follows:

'You looked so peaceful I hadn't the heart to wake you. Have gone shopping, but back in an hour. No hurry to get up. Love J.'

There was one rather annoying omission in this message, insofar as it did not specify the time of its composition, but I deduced from the temperature of the coffee that it could not have been there for more than twenty minutes and, with the whole house to myself and more than half an hour in hand, this was plainly a chance in a million to embark on the next move.

I used up another five minutes in fortifying myself with some tepid coffee and a slice of flabby toast, while pulling on slacks and a jersey, and before leaving the room had the foresight to look out of the window which faced over the drive. There was a black Jaguar parked near the front door, which did not prove anything because this was a six-car family if ever I met one, but it did convey the warning that Julie's shopping expedition might have been postponed and that she was still in the house. I therefore stood in the gallery for several minutes, leaning down over the rail and repeatedly calling her name. There was no answer, nor any sound at all from the cavernous depths, and as a last precaution I padded along to her bedroom and tapped on the door. Absolute silence here too, and I turned the handle and looked inside. There was no one there, but both beds were made up and on each set of pillows there was a collection of teddy bears, woolly dogs and bunny rabbits. It was rather a saddening sight and, as I shut the door, it occurred to me, not for the first time, that Kit was probably well out of it.

My next call was only a few yards away and the door was unlocked. Nothing, at first glance, had changed since I was last there but only one object required close attention and to reach it I had to pass by the archway leading to the dressing room and private gymnasium, and then turn into the L section of the bedroom.

The desk top was clear of papers, with only a massive silver inkstand and the two telephones on its vast polished surface. I stationed myself in front of it, my hands clasping the back of the swivel chair, and my eyes almost on a level with those of the woman in the portrait. There was something insipid and yet appealing in her expression, and I remained riveted to it for several minutes after verifying what I had come to find out. I was about to turn away at last when a prickling sensation at the back of my neck warned me of the presence of someone standing just behind me. Cold with shock and fear, unable to speak or move, I clenched my hands tighter round the chair and heard a voice say softly:

'Interesting portrait, isn't it?'

The fact that it was the voice I had expected to hear partially broke the spell. It cost an enormous effort, but at least I was able to turn round and meet the cruel, mad eyes, and this small achievement raised my morale one notch higher still. The power of speech gradually returned and I said, in as steady a voice as I could manage:

'She must have been extremely beautiful?'

'Oh, she was. Beautiful and cheap and wanton, as you've no doubt gathered. How nice to see you again, incidentally! I am so glad you consented to come.'

For some absurd reason, these incongruously conventional remarks started a fresh panic, and I became obsessed with the fear that he would ask me if I was enjoying myself. To stave off a rising hysteria, I cut in quickly:

'I'm sure you must wonder what I'm doing in your room, but I was passing the door when I thought I heard the telephone. I didn't realise you were back and Julie's out shopping, so I thought I'd better answer it.'

He shook his head sadly. 'No, my dear, I'm afraid that won't do. These telephones don't have bells, just a little buzz, which can't be heard from outside. I should like to believe you, I really would. It quite dismays me to find you're a liar, on top of everything else; but I have to tell you that the only part of your statement which rings true is that you had not realised I was back.'

Still striving against all the odds to cool this down to a normal level, I said:

'Well, it is rather a surprise, isn't it? I'm sure Julie can't have been expecting you, or she'd have told me.'

'Which is precisely why I didn't inform her of my intentions. However, when I spoke to her on the telephone yesterday and she mentioned that you were coming to stay I thought it would be advisable to find out why. I never like to neglect details, as you know.'

'Rather a trivial one, surely, to warrant so much time and trouble? Why shouldn't I come and stay with her when she'd invited me to?'

'I must confess I find that inadequate. Poor Julie is not over-bright, as you know. A little more credulous than you and me, and I daresay that story would do very well for her. But I think you and I are rather alike in some ways, don't you?'

I forced back the instinctive denial, for it struck me just in time that he might not after all be perfectly sure of his ground and was trying to needle me into committing myself in some way.

'Perhaps so,' I replied indifferently.

'Ah, you agree? I'm glad of that because you'll probably understand that I'm not being melodramatic when I suggest that the world is too small to accommodate both of us?'

Once more, I tried to appear unmoved. I realised only too well that the pretence had become something of a farce but presumably, when confronted with a lunatic, any strategy is better than none at all.

'No, I wouldn't go all the way with you there, Magnus. I've apologised for being in your room, and it's not really such a crime, is it?'

'A crime? Oh dear me, no, I should think not. More of a coincidence is how I should put it. A coincidence which I was fortunate enough to have foreseen.'

'What does it coincide with?'

'A good question. The answer is: far too many things for my comfort. To name a few which spring to mind, it was you who discovered poor Sarah.'

'Kit and me together.'

'Oh, and Kit too, as you say; but it was you, if memory serves, who insisted on leaving her in the tent? Moreover, I understand that you were at Missendale within half an hour of Babs Graham's death?'

'There was no plan about that either; just a fluke.'

'Indeed? And was it just a fluke that you were actively engaged on the African boy's behalf, even to the extent of hiring a clever legal gentleman to take up his case? Oh yes, my dear, I know all about that. I am not without influence when it comes to checking on people's activities. However, enough of that, we haven't got all the time in the world. Julie may be back from her shopping at any moment.'

'Does Julie know you're here?' I asked, striving to keep a spark of hope out of my voice.

'Certainly she does. I could hardly keep my arrival secret from her, could I? She was a little worried about leaving you, but I said I was perfectly capable of entertaining you until she returned. I even invented a little errand to Missendale which I hoped she might undertake. And I'm not in the least worried about Julie, you know. If she does return and find you gone, she will merely conclude that you are out for a stroll or something. She won't break in on us here, I promise you. She may not be so bright as her poor sister, but she does surpass her in obedience, and I have given strict instructions that I am not be disturbed.'

'You're mad,' I said. 'Absolutely raving. I've suspected it for some time, but this clinches it.'

'By some standards, that may be true,' he replied equably, 'but it can hardly bring you much consolation. If I am mad, what chance have you of deflecting me with your so-called sane arguments? My mind is quite made up and nothing will alter it.'

'But even you must see that you wouldn't have a hope of getting away with it. Your influence doesn't extend that far.'

'You're thinking, I daresay, that I may have some trouble in accounting for your disappearance?' he asked, still speaking with the utmost civility, as though we were discussing some abstract problem, which I found even more demoralising than if he had ranted like a lunatic and which, I also felt sure, was his intention.

'Exactly. Even if you could fool Julie indefinitely, which I strongly doubt, there are numerous other people who would start asking questions.'

'Are there? I wonder? Julie, of course, is a separate case. Poor child, she misses Sarah so dreadfully, I live in constant fear that it may drive her to suicide one of these days. However, let us consider these numerous people. I take it your husband and cousin know where you are?'

I nodded, though evidently not putting as much conviction into it as I had hoped, for he looked more complacent than ever.

'Even so, could they actually prove that you came? I flatter myself that I have summed you up accurately, as a headstrong, not always truthful young person, so they may not be hard to convince that, having announced one set of plans, you then embarked on another. Horrified, grief stricken, naturally, but not incredulous.'

'Nevertheless, there is plenty of evidence to show that I did come.'

'Again, I would question it. As you may have noticed, I had the forethought to put it to Julie that it would be only fair to give our staff some time off while you were here to keep her company; and in fact she went one better. So eager to please, poor child, that she sent them all packing without giving any instructions for preparing your room. She was quite distressed about it this morning. Apparently they hadn't even remade the bed since your last visit.'

'There is still my car,' I reminded him, clutching at every straw to keep the dialogue flowing. 'You may have some difficulty in explaining how it comes to be in your garage.'

'Ah, the car! Thank you for reminding me. Not that I was in much danger of forgetting it. It's an integral part of my plan, you see. When you do turn up, in two or three days, or whatever it may be, you will be found inside the wreckage of your own car. Quite a neat scheme, don't you agree?'

Without any warning, I suddenly found myself in the grip of the most extraordinary lassitude. Perhaps the unequal struggle of sparring with this bombastic, murdering maniac had sapped every last ounce of vitality, but what I experienced most strongly at this point was not so much fear as utter fatigue. I instinctively moved away from the claustrophobic L shaped enclosure, in search of purer air, and sat down on the bed. Whereupon, to my horror and amazement, I opened my mouth and yawned, like some great overfed, lazy cat.

For the first time, Magnus was truly disconcerted. Some ridiculous reflex action had caused me to turn my head, to apologise for all I know, and I clearly saw a fleeting expression of uncertainty in his eyes. For the moment I had the upper hand and, to gain time wherein to consider how to use it, I repeated the yawn, but in a more genteel form, patting my mouth with my fingers as though to admonish myself for bad manners. No gesture could have been more inspired, as it turned out, for my features were already so distorted by this carry-on that I was certain that no flicker of emotion was transmitted to Magnus when, over the top of my fingers, I saw the door knob moving back and forth. A second later a figure slid silently into view, and then passed like a shadow through the archway to the dressing room. The significance of this escaped me utterly, apart from vague forebodings of fresh trouble for myself. I bent down and pretended to search in my bag for a tissue while struggling to work out all the new implications.

'I am sorry if I bore you,' Magnus said.

Although it felt like six times as long, probably not more than two minutes had elapsed since he had last spoken, and hope see-sawed up again as I recognised the involuntary irritation in his tone. It swung higher still when, staring straight ahead of me in what I hoped would pass for an attitude of deep thought or total indifference, I saw no movement from the dressing room intruder and a new revelation broke over me.

'I suppose you really hated Sarah?' I enquired, coming out of my reverie.

"Nothing of the sort. She was extremely useful to me, and I became quite attached to her in the latter years.'

'Then how could you bear to . . . ?'

'She got in my way, you see, just as you have, and that's something I won't tolerate.'

'And did your wife get in your way too, or was that a genuine death from natural causes?' I asked, still striving to keep it on a chatty level, which any sane person would have found somewhat inappropriate to the theme.

'Yes, indeed it was. She was a feeble creature, you know, not unlike Julie; and always picking up every ailment that was going. In that climate, of course, it was largely a question of time. She hated the Middle East, and she was rather unhappy, for various reasons. That may have contributed to her death, I daresay.'

'What I can't understand,' I said ruminatively but at the same time nice and loud for the benefit of the hidden listener, 'is why, when you found out the truth, you didn't simply divorce her and start afresh. Why did the canker have to go on festering until it got too big to handle, to coin a phrase or two?'

'My dear girl, isn't it obvious? She had humiliated me; deeply and unforgivably. But at least it remained private between ourselves. Divorce would have made it common property. A public humiliation! Besides, that family of hers would have opened their arms to her and the children in no time. It was what she wanted, and I wasn't having it. She had to be punished, not rewarded.'

'But Sarah was made of sterner stuff, I take it? When she discovered that you were behind the Clean Up Crusade, you couldn't whip her into submission? She was implacable and she had to go. Is that how it was?'

'It should never have been necessary,' he replied with a hint of petulance. 'It was the most shocking luck that she got on to it at all, and I tried my best to make her see that it doesn't always pay to wear your heart on your sleeve in politics. The end justifies the means very often, and anyway I should never have got where I am if I hadn't hedged my bets. The trouble was that she'd inherited all these high falutin notions about integrity and so on. She hated to be disloyal; I could tell that, but she'd begun to dither. I recognised all the signs, and that interview I had with Walter on Good Friday, when you'd all gone to Missendale, was the last straw. How was I to know that Sarah would leave the party and come racing home on her own?'

'Yes, very tactless of her,' I agreed. 'But what about Babs? How had she managed to upset your apple cart?'

'Oh, didn't you know?' he asked. 'Funny! I thought you had all the answers.'

Knocked off guard by his change of tone, I jerked my head round and saw that he had laid a paper knife across his knee and was running his finger along its slender, hideously sharp looking blade.

'So!' he said, meeting my look and smiling his detestable smile. 'After all, there are some things you will go to your grave without discovering. I find that rather heartening. And I want you to know, my dear, that I am perfectly aware of the motive behind all these questions. You have been hoping, have you not, to divert me with your chatter until the miracle arrives to save your skin? I've indulged you, up to a point, because it rather amuses me to watch the fish struggling on the hook; but enough is enough, and it's beginning to bore me now.'

'I quite agree with you,' I said, getting up and moving as slowly as I dared towards the door. 'My own sentiments exactly.'

He caught up with me in a flash. I could feel his presence close behind me and then the point of the knife between my shoulder blades.

'That won't do you any good, my poor girl, I don't neglect details, you know, and that door is locked.'

'Oh no, it ain't,' Walter said, emerging from his hiding place at last, and shooting out a nice muscular right arm.

It was really a pushover, in every sense, for one of his training on the football field. The adversary was taken completely by surprise and in a moment the knife had dropped to the floor with a thud. There followed a louder and, to my ears, still more musical thud, and when I looked round I saw that Magnus had gone the same way. He was sitting on the floor, with his legs stretched out in front of him, while Walter appeared to be tying his arms into a knot behind his back.

'You took your time,' I said crossly.

He looked up at me, scarlet in the face from remorse or exertion, his adam's apple jerking convulsively.

'Well, he was talking a blue streak, and you seemed to be doing fine, so I—hey, listen! You okay, Mrs Price?'

'I'm not sure whether I am or not,' I replied in a voice which seemed to be coming from mid-Atlantic. 'I feel strangely wonky. And I'm warning you, Walter, if there's any fainting to be done, it's me who will . . .'

At which point, as I afterwards learnt, I keeled over and joined the rest of the party on the floor.

CHAPTER SIXTEEN

'AT LEAST, he claims I said that,' I explained later. 'And it shows how far my tether had run out. Otherwise, I expect I'd have said: "It is I who shall . . ." Unless, of course, he was paraphrasing that bit. Walter is a wonderful boy in many ways but not so hot on the English grammar.'

'It is a pity he did not reveal himself in his wonderful colours a littler earlier,' Robin remarked. 'It might have saved a lot of misunderstanding.'

Not for the first time, at the conclusion of an eventful period in our lives, he and I and Toby were spending the evening together, reminiscing about various matters which had stirred us up during the preceding weeks.

'I know, Robin, but the trouble was that he was playing a lone hand and most of the time he did everything completely wrong. Just occasionally he brought off a real coup, though. I mean, imagine guessing there was something bogus about that errand of Julie's to Missendale and then pinching her Jag! I probably owe my life to that moment of inspiration. If only I'd realised he was an ally! But my big mistake was in marking him down from the start as a natural for the Clean Up brigade. Poor Walter, he was just as much a victim of prejudice as Henry, in a way. If I hadn't fallen into that trap I'd have got to the real reason for all the silly lies he told and we should have known where we were.'

'Speak for yourself,' Toby said. 'I shouldn't have known where I was, and I still don't. How about you, Robin?'

'Well, I understand why he lied to Tessa about having spent the whole morning at the Potteries when she turned up there with her celebrated slow puncture. It appears that he had seized the chance to nip over and visit his girl friend in Oxford, and was too scared to own up to it, specially after racing round a bend on the wrong side and knocking down his master potter. It was then that he got the bright idea of ditching the bike and pretending that it had been stolen.'

'Not to mention his equally misguided attempt to thwart the murderer's intentions by removing the note from the golf club. But he started his trail of confusion long before that. It began when I was trying to find Magnus to tell him that Sarah was dead. Walter came out of the downstairs cloakroom and said he'd tried to make a telephone call, but he'd heard Magnus on the line, and that was how he knew he was upstairs in his room. A foolish blunder, because if I hadn't been so stupefied with shock I'd have remembered that Magnus's telephones were on separate lines, not connected to any other part of the house. By the time I caught on, it had become irrelevant.'

Robin said: 'Not all that irrelevant, surely? It might have occurred to you that Walter had gone to the cloakroom to wash the blood off his hands?'

'Yes, it might, but you see I was so stuck on this idea that he was operating on Magnus's instructions, and it was inconceivable that anyone could be such a monster as to manipulate the murder of his own daughter. It was the same hang up which got in the way when everything began to point to Magnus himself being the murderer.'

'In any case,' Toby reminded us, 'it was just as Walter said. Magnus was in his room, was he not?'

'Yes, he was. All that build up about how much he was going to enjoy the fête fooled me completely, with the result that the house was the last place where I'd thought of looking for him. So I wasted ages searching in all the wrong places, and it was time which, as you know, he was putting to good use.'

'Disposing of the evidence, no doubt?'

'Yes, he was over at Missendale dumping the stained overall in the kiln. I'm not sure how he got hold of it in the first place, but I expect it was quite easy. He may even have pinched it off the washing line. I happen to know the laundry was done on the premises.'

'Tessa really does collect the most extraordinary information, doesn't she, Robin? Not so much a mine as a jumble sale really.'

'I merely happened to notice it hanging out to dry,' I said huffily. 'It coincided with the other discovery, of a corpse in the car, so it didn't impinge at the time. And, incidentally, Magnus didn't dispose of the weapon, along with the overall. He may have realised that metal doesn't completely disintegrate, even at white heat and that it could have been traced to him. It was always his proud boast that he didn't neglect details. Unfortunately for him, though, there was one detail which he did leave out of his calculations and that was Walter's late arrival at the fête. Even the ticket seller at the gate had packed up by then, so he was able to slide in unobtrusively and while he was parking his bike on the grass he saw Magnus drive in, and he tailed him into the house. Then he heard someone coming and bolted into the cloakroom, but he came out again when he heard me shouting for Magnus, because he could tell it was urgent, and he made the first excuse he could think of for knowing where Magnus was.'

'But why was he tailing him at all?' Toby asked. 'Principally because he'd guessed there was something fishy about the brick throwing episode. I gather he'd had doubts about Magnus's sincerity for some time, but that finally did it.'

'Did what?'

I paused for a while before answering, for we had reached a point in the narrative which called for a some-what humbling admission on my part, and the words did not flow so smoothly. When Toby had repeated the question I said:

'If I hadn't been such a coward, things might have turned out differently. Unfortunately, I mistook the brick for a bomb and I had my head under a cushion at the vital period. When I did look up, Magnus was on his knees in the middle of the room. I assumed he'd crawled there, after being struck, in a gallant attempt to catch the assailant; but the point was, and Walter saw it, that he'd moved into that position before, not after the brick was slung.'

'On purpose?'

'Right. And mainly for Sarah's benefit. Walter had started the rot by hinting to her about Magnus's double identity, and she'd finally nerved herself to ask him straight out if it was true. He denied it categorically and then worked out this plan to demonstrate that the Cleaners really had got it in for him. He even ordered her to read the note aloud, so that all present would literally get the message. That didn't quite work out though, so he carefully threw it down in a spot where anyone who was interested could pick it up and read it.'

'But Sarah wasn't taken in by all this fandango?'

'Perhaps not. I think it threw her into an even worse turmoil of indecision. But Walter had seen through it, and he took action. Instead of going straight to Oxford to meet his girl friend on Good Friday, he visited Eglinton Hall on the way. Knowing that the rest of us were safely off the premises,

Magnus interviewed him in the drawing room, where I don't need to remind you there was a broken window overlooking the lawn. They had a fairly acrimonious discussion, which concluded with Walter being told that if he didn't shut up and mind his own business his grant would be stopped and he'd be sent home. This put him in a proper fix because, apart from being dedicated to his pots, he's also potty about this girl of his.'

'Poor lad! What a difficult life he has.'

'Anyway, he gave Magnus a few to get on with and then barged out of the room in such a flaming rage that he damn near bashed into Kit's car as we were coming in. But what neither of them had realised was that every word of their quarrel had been overheard by Sarah. She left us at the Potteries because she wanted to keep an eye on Magnus, but the first thing she did was to mark out the spot where Madame Rosetta's tent was to be put up, and that's how she happened to be standing beside the broken window. After that, of course, Magnus hadn't a hope of convincing her, and he had to resort to drastic measures. Incidentally, the window wasn't broken intentionally. It was partly my fault that it happened.'

'Only partly? Oh, Tessa, what an admission!'

'Well, the accomplice must take some of the praise or blame.'

'Ah yes, the accomplice!' Robin said, breaking a long silence. 'He fooled you, didn't he? Perhaps he was a better actor than you ever gave him credit for?'

'You're talking of Kitbag?' Toby asked in great astonishment.

'Yes, he was another of those loonies who secretly subscribed to the Aryan aristocracy theory and all the rest of it. And he was completely under Magnus's thumb, financially as well as ideologically. He'd been taken to My Leader and found him just the ticket.'

'Well, you do surprise me, and I have to agree with Robin. I think he may have a great future on the stage, after all.'

'Well, I don't, because ultimately he ruins the effect by overacting and that's very difficult to eradicate. I was puzzled all along by how excessively drunk he got that evening. Normally he could put away several quarts without turning a hair, and it wasn't as though he'd been at it all day. Yet by half past nine he was completely stoned. It was all according to instructions, but he laid it on far too thick.'

'What instructions?'

'That everyone should see how drunk he was and find it quite natural for him to stumble out into the night air. His job was then to grab the brick, which had been planted in a convenient spot and, on a signal from Magnus, to toss it through the open window. Later, he was to come bursting in, all dishevelled and emotional, with the news that he'd seen a bunch of desperados making off towards the meadow, but hadn't been steady enough to give chase. But it didn't go according to the script. He overdid the act and it ended with my escorting him into the garden. He did his best to shake me off, and eventually I went indoors again, but shut the window behind me, which gummed up the works considerably. Throwing the brick through glass made it doubly tricky, and in fact I don't think it struck Magnus at all. I believe he picked up a sliver of glass in his handkerchief and dug it into his forehead to get the blood flowing. Anyway, the scar looked much more like a cut of that type, because there were no bruises or swelling, as Dr Simmons confirmed when I put it to him.'

'And you mean that Walter saw all this at the time?'

'Not exactly. He's impulsive, as they all kept telling me, and it was a natural reflex for him to go flying off in pursuit. There was no one there, of course, except Kit, who had flung himself down on the grass, and Walter put two and two together and weighed in with the left hook. He's inclined to act first and think later.'

'But surely Sarah must also have realised that the cut hadn't been made by a brick?'

'I expect so; and that's why Magnus had to pile it on with fake headaches and loss of appetite and so on. Though, mind you, he had a different version for his loyal public. He pretended to us that it was necessary to hush up the affair, but in fact he went dancing about in full view of several hundred people, including press photographers, with a wodge of totally unnecessary surgical dressings on his head. And that, I believe, is what led to Babs' downfall.'

'Oh? Had she seen through it too?'

'No, but I think she found this lump of lint and sticking plaster inside the tent. Presumably it fell off when he attacked Sarah and Babs automatically scooped it up and popped it in her bag. Later on, she may have found that Magnus had no intention of leading her to the altar, so either she decided to go for some money instead, or maybe she just enjoyed having some kind of hold over him. The plaster was a perfect weapon for blackmail because he'd been so busy pressing it back into place all the afternoon that it must have been covered with his fingerprints.'

'I rather fancied Babs as the murderer at one time,' Toby remarked wistfully. 'And I rather wish she had been.'

'Me too; specially as she had the best opportunity for shoving Henry's overall in the kiln. And, having been married to a doctor, she probably knew a lot about how to kill people. Furthermore, I'd worked out a splendid motive for her. She longed for Sarah to get married and leave the field clear for herself and when she found that the marriage wouldn't change the set up, everything seemed to fall into place. I'd discounted Magnus at that time because I didn't know all the facts and I was bogged down by the idea that no man could be such a monster as to kill his own daughter.'

'According to his statement,' Robin said, 'he put his head through the back of the tent and asked Sarah to make some excuse to leave her crystal ball for five minutes, as he had something urgent to discuss with her. He then withdrew and waited outside, meaning to strike her down as she came out; but he had a stroke of luck in that the next client was Babs and he heard Sarah telling her to keep everyone at bay while she went to the bathroom. That gave Magnus a marvellous opportunity to step inside and do the job on the spot.'

'Poor old Babs!' I said. 'If only she'd left well alone she'd have been in no danger, but she had to go and complicate things by trying to cash in. Magnus no doubt tried every trick there was to con her into believing that he'd dropped the sticking plaster at some other time, but all the same you'd have expected her to be a bit wary of him. Instead of which, when he pretended that his car wasn't ready, and suggested their lunching together at Missendale, she not only agreed, but took good care that her husband shouldn't be present.'

'Yes, it was rather reckless, but she may have been relying on Walter to protect her if things got rough. Perhaps the discovery that his motor bike had gone gave her such a jolt that she gave the game away and Magnus realised that there wasn't another soul on the premises. After that, she hadn't a chance.'

'And so, having done his double bluff with the note on the golf club, all that remained,' I said, 'was to nip through the back of the Potteries and across the fields to the Eglinton Garage, where his car was waiting.'

'Yes, and that's the part which defeats me utterly,' Toby complained. 'Robin told us categorically that it was Babs who drove him to the garage, and furthermore that the petrol pump man saw her drive away again, alive and well.'

'He thought he did,' I explained. 'It was a genuine mistake, but so often people see a certain amount with their eyes and fill in the gaps with their imagination. If I were to walk behind your chair now and go over to the bookcase, at the same time remarking that there was a lion in your garden, I bet you anything that in describing the event afterwards you'd say that I was looking out of the window.'

'I don't see what that's got to do with it,' he replied crossly. 'The point is that this man wasn't sitting in a chair with his back to them.'

'No, but the principle is the same. What he actually saw was Magnus walking up the forecourt to his car, getting in and checking the ignition for a bit, and then finally waving and tooting his horn to a female who drove past on the other side of the road. His mind filled in all the rest, including the fiction that Babs, having turned her car round in the interval, was the woman. How was he to know that Magnus deliberately sat there, fiddling with the controls until a nondescript vehicle with a woman driver appeared in his sights? But I guessed it could have happened in that way and I did some checking up. The mechanic who changed my wheel vaguely knew the Grahams by sight, but they're not regular customers and he wasn't even sure what make of car they owned.'

'Tessa's right,' Robin said. 'It's a curious thing, but the petrol pump attendant could only give the haziest description of the car the woman was driving; on the other hand, he was absolutely positive that she and Magnus knew each other.'

'All the same Mag was taking a big risk, wasn't he?'

'He believed in taking risks,' I reminded them. 'In fact, he told me the first time I met him that his worst mistakes had come from being over-cautious. And he had such sublime faith in his own powers that it probably never occurred to him that anything he undertook could go wrong. Being so athletic was a help too; that canter across the fields was a mere bagatelle. On the whole, one must concede that he made very few mistakes.'

'Except in his marriage, of course.'

'Oh yes, that was the real failure. And how it rankled! That a woman so blessed by fortune as to become his wife should dare to be unfaithful to him, and then to flaunt her infidelity with two little black eyed strangers! I wonder why Sarah and Julie never caught on?'

'Well, children rarely question these things, luckily for their parents.'

'But apart from his very unpaternal attitude, the most conspicuous thing about Magnus was the colour of his eyes; like the sea in the early morning light. Neither of the girls had inherited them, nor their mother's either. I had to go back for another look at the portrait to confirm it, but I was fairly certain that hers were blue.'

'Does that prove anything?' Toby asked, looking rather worried.

'Apparently, it does. It was one of the facts I prised out of Dr Simmons. He was cagey at first, but he finally admitted that although Sarah and Julie were naturally in the same blood group, Magnus belonged to a different one. That wasn't conclusive, but he also agreed, on purely hypothetical terms, that it's virtually unknown for a brown eyed child to be born of two blue eyed parents. It showed me plainly that one could not rule out the concept of Magnus as the murderer, because not only was Sarah unrelated to him, but to a man of his temperament her mere existence would always have been a thorn in the flesh. Perhaps in killing her he was finally revenging himself, in some twisted way, on her mother.'

'Well, I'm staggered, aren't you, Robin? Imagine Tessa being so well up in genetics, on top of everything else! Whatever would the C.I.D. do without her?'

'Oh, they'd have caught up with Magnus sooner or later,' I told him. 'A bombastic, conceited man like him was bound to give himself away eventually. It's like I always say; in the end people are brought down by their own weaknesses. Magnus, for instance, was always going on about his wonderful grasp of detail, but it was more of an Achilles heel in some ways.'

Robin frowned. 'Why do you say that? If he'd simply concentrated on the little detail of not giving himself away it might have worked out splendidly.'

'But he would inevitably have tripped himself up at some stage. That's my point, and to illustrate it I'll give you an example. When he was yapping away to me in his bedroom, with the knife in his hands, he couldn't resist accusing me, among other crimes, of having arrived at Missendale only half an hour after Babs was killed. It was a detail, right enough, and it was also a complete giveaway. Anyone could have found out what time I arrived there; only the murderer would have known whether it was half an hour, or two minutes after the event.'

'You have removed a weight from my mind,' Toby said gravely. 'What a relief to know that if you ever give up detection the course of justice may be slowed down, but it needn't necessarily come to a halt. So I suppose the only one left to worry about now is poor Miss Julie?'

'Don't call her that. She hates it, and on the whole it's not appropriate. Despite everything, Julie has quite a lot going for her. She has no blood ties with the murderer, but on the other hand I bet he's already settled vast chunks of money on her.'

'There is a saying to the effect that money can't buy me love.'

'I am aware of it, Toby, but I also happen to know that Dr Simmons is a bachelor, and he could certainly do with a softening influence in his life. Then there's poor lonely Martin, sorely in need of some home comforts, and Julie is quite a passable cook. However, on the whole I think it would be best if she married Kit.'

'You can't be serious? I can think of nothing more tedious.'

'Neither can I, but he worships money, and Julie is conditioned to these bull-dozing reactionary types. And he has one great pull over all the other prince charmings, which I bet hasn't occurred to either of you.'

'I bet it hasn't either,' Robin admitted sadly.

'Well, just think! They could jog along together for ever and ever, and it wouldn't make the slightest difference what colour the children's eyes were.'

THE END

FELICITY SHAW

THE detective novels of Anne Morice seem rather to reflect the actual life and background of the author, whose full married name was Felicity Anne Morice Worthington Shaw. Felicity was born in the county of Kent on February 18, 1916, one of four daughters of Harry Edward Worthington, a well-loved village doctor, and his pretty young wife, Muriel Rose Morice. Seemingly this is an unexceptional provenance for an English mystery writer—yet in fact Felicity's complicated ancestry was like something out of a classic English mystery, with several cases of children born on the wrong side of the blanket to prominent sires and their humbly born paramours. Her mother Muriel Rose was the natural daughter of dressmaker Rebecca Garnett Gould and Charles John Morice, a Harrow graduate and footballer who played in the 1872 England/Scotland match. Doffing his football kit after this triumph, Charles became a stockbroker like his father, his brothers and his nephew Percy John de Paravicini, son of Baron James Prior de Paravicini and Charles' only surviving sister, Valentina Antoinette Sampayo Morice. (Of Scottish mercantile origin, the Morices had extensive Portuguese business connections.) Charles also found time, when not playing the fields of sport or commerce, to father a pair of out-of-wedlock children with a coachman's daughter, Clementina Frances Turvey, whom he would later marry.

Her mother having passed away when she was only four years old, Muriel Rose was raised by her half-sister Kitty, who had wed a commercial traveler, at the village of Birchington-on-Sea, Kent, near the city of Margate. There she met kindly local doctor Harry Worthington when he treated her during a local measles outbreak. The case of measles led to marriage between the physician and his patient, with the couple wedding in 1904, when Harry was thirty-six and Muriel Rose but twenty-two. Together Harry and Muriel Rose had a daughter, Elizabeth, in 1906. However Muriel Rose's three later daughters—Angela, Felicity and Yvonne—were fathered by another man, London playwright Frederick Leonard Lonsdale, the author of such popular stage works (many of them adapted as films) as *On Approval* and *The Last of Mrs. Cheyney* as well as being the most steady of Muriel Rose's many lovers.

Unfortunately for Muriel Rose, Lonsdale's interest in her evaporated as his stage success mounted. The playwright proposed pensioning off his discarded mistress with an annual stipend of one hundred pounds apiece for each of his natural daughters, provided that he and Muriel Rose never met again. The offer was accepted, although Muriel Rose, a woman of golden flights and fancies who romantically went by the name Lucy Glitters (she told her daughters that her father had christened her with this appellation on account of his having won a bet on a horse by that name on the day she was born), never got over the rejection. Meanwhile, "poor Dr. Worthington" as he was now known, had come down with Parkinson's Disease and he was packed off with a nurse to a cottage while "Lucy Glitters," now in straitened financial circumstances by her standards, moved with her daughters to a maisonette above a cake shop in Belgravia, London, in a bid to get the girls established. Felicity's older sister Angela went into acting for a profession, and her mother's theatrical ambition for her daughter is said to have been the inspiration for Noel Coward's amusingly imploring 1935 hit song "Don't Put Your Daughter on the Stage, Mrs. Worthington." Angela's greatest contribution to the cause of thespianism by far came when she married actor and theatrical agent Robin Fox, with whom she produced England's Fox acting dynasty, including her sons Edward and James and grandchildren Laurence, Jack, Emilia and Freddie.

Felicity meanwhile went to work in the office of the GPO Film Unit, a subdivision of the United Kingdom's General Post Office established in 1933 to produce documentary films. Her daughter Mary Premila Boseman has written that it was at the GPO Film Unit that the "pretty and fashionably slim" Felicity met documentarian Alexander Shaw—"good looking, strong featured, dark haired and with strange brown eyes between yellow and green"—and told herself "that's the man I'm going to marry," which she did. During the Thirties and Forties Alex produced and/or directed over a score of prestige documentaries, including *Tank Patrol*, *Our Country* (introduced by actor Burgess Meredith) and *Penicillin*. After World War Two Alex worked with the United Nations agencies UNESCO and UNRWA and he and Felicity and their three children resided in developing nations all around the world. Felicity's daughter Mary recalls that Felicity "set up house in most of these places adapting to each circumstance. Furniture and curtains and so on were made of local materials. . . . The only possession that followed us everywhere from England was the box of Christmas decorations, practically heirlooms, fragile and attractive and unbroken throughout. In Wad Medani in the Sudan they hung on a thorn bush and looked charming."

It was during these years that Felicity began writing fiction, eventually publishing two fine mainstream novels, *The Happy Exiles* (1956) and *Sun-Trap* (1958). The former novel, a lightly satirical comedy of manners about British and American expatriates in an unnamed British colony during the dying days of the Empire, received particularly good reviews and was published in both the United Kingdom and the United States, but after a nasty bout with malaria and the death, back in England, of her mother Lucy Glitters, Felicity put writing aside for more than a decade, until under her pseudonym Anne Morice, drawn from her two middle names, she successfully launched her Tessa Crichton mystery series in 1970. "From the royalties of these books," notes Mary Premila Boseman, "she was able to buy a house in Hambleden, near Henley-on-Thames; this was the first of our houses that wasn't rented." Felicity spent a great deal more time in the home country during the last two decades of her life, gardening and cooking for friends (though she herself when alone subsisted on a diet of black coffee and watercress) and industriously spinning her tales of genteel English murder in locales much like that in which she now resided. Sometimes she joined Alex in his overseas travels to different places, including Washington, D.C., which she wrote about with characteristic wryness in her 1977 detective novel *Murder with Mimicry* ("a nice lively book saturated with show business," pronounced the *New York Times Book Review*). Felicity Shaw lived a full life of richly varied experiences, which are rewardingly reflected in her books, the last of which was published posthumously in 1990, a year after her death at the age of seventy-three on May 18th, 1989.

Curtis Evans

CPSIA information can be obtained
at www.ICGtesting.com
Printed in the USA
LVHW022318220321
682109LV00010B/201